WILDFIRE

TWO

WILD *Duet*

AN ASHFORD FAMILY NOVEL

D.M. DAVIS

Copyright © 2022 D.M. Davis

WILDFIRE by D.M. Davis
WILD Duet Book Two
Published by D.M. Davis

ISBN: 979-8-9869509-2-1

www.dmckdavis.com
Cover Design by D.M. Davis
Cover Photo by Depositphotos
Editing by Tamara Mataya
Proofreading by Mountains Wanted Publishing & Indie Author Services
Formatting by Champagne Book Design

ABOUT THIS BOOK

D.M. Davis' **WILDFIRE** is the continuation of Reid and Daisy's angsty, break your heart, first responder, steamy contemporary romance and Book Two in the *Wild* Duet.

After a year of secret crushes and weekly visits
under false pretenses,
I finally have my Wildflower.
She's everything I've always wanted and then some.
My heart is full.
Life is good.
Our future is within reach.

In a flash, our lives go up in flames.
I'm forced to make an impossible life or death decision—one I'm
not sure we can come back from.
There was no choice.
I'd give my last breath to save my Daisy.
I nearly did.

In the aftermath, it wasn't only her apartment and
shop that were decimated.
I destroyed her trust, her faith, and possibly her love.
I smashed it all over a secret and a sacrifice she wasn't
prepared to live with.

But here's the thing: I'd do it all again.
I don't regret a single second, other than hurting her.
Even if it means I have to live with this hole in my
heart—in my life—forever…

Some choices are nearly impossible to come back from.

Intended for mature audiences.

PLAYLIST

Beneath Your Beautiful by Labrinth

Bed on Fire by Teddy Swims

Queen of California by John Mayer

Glimpse of Us by Joji

Sometimes I Cry by Chris Stapleton

Sucker by Jonas Brothers

July by Noah Cyrus

Till We Both Say by Nicotine Dolls

Need You Now by Micky

Iris by The Goo Goo Dolls

911 by Teddy Swims

Who Says You Can't Go Home by Bon Jovi & Jennifer Nettles

Like I'm Gonna Lose You by Micky

The Story by Brandi Carlile

At My Worst by Will Gittens & Kayla Rae

Quietly Yours by Birdy

Amazing by Teddy Swims

WILDFIRE

Disclaimer

This is a work of fiction, straight from my heart. Please extend grace to any inaccuracies. While trying to honor the brave men and women who protect us from such tragedies, I took some creative liberties for the sake of the story. In no way did I meant any disrespect to these real-life heroes and the people who love them.

DEDICATION

For Kinsley

CHAPTER 1

I'M DREAMING OF SWEET WILDFLOWERS AND my Daisy. It must be a dream, for the way her heat is gripping my cock can't be real, considering we didn't actually have sex last night. It was close. Very. Very. Close. But—

"Oh, my God. Reid!" Small but determined hands shake me.

Zero to sixty, I pop awake and frown at the fear in her eyes. "Flower?" Instinct has me taking a deeper breath, scenting the air. *Fuck.* I sit up, holding her so I don't accidentally knock her on her ass. "Fire."

She points to the bedroom door. "I think my apartment's on fire."

The tremble in her voice has me jumping into action. "Get dressed."

As I pull on my clothes and shoes, I assess our situation, eyeing the *only* window in the room, and move closer to the door. I don't need to touch it to know there are flames entirely too close to escape that way. The heat is radiating from it with a warm glow, like heaven is on the other side when, in fact, it's hell.

Keep calm. Stay alive. Save her.

Keep calm. Stay alive.

Save her.

Backing away, I take in Daisy dressing, measuring her reaction to my level of concern. Her hands shake as she watches me.

Keep calm. Stay alive. Save her.

I grab the top sheet from the bed and stuff it in the crack at the bottom of the door, making a mental note to pour water on it if we have enough left. I head for her closet, dialing 9-1-1 as I begin to fill the duffel bag I find on the top shelf with clothes. I want to be thorough, picking what she'll need, but really, I'm grabbing and shoving, barely taking time to see what's in my hands before moving to another section, praying, praying the fire will never get this close. By the crackling and burning on the other side of her door, I'm not sure how much time I have to save her, much less her things. One bag is better than nothing.

When the operator answers, I identify myself, report the fire, give Daisy's address, and *then* call my brother.

He answers on the first ring. "Reid?"

"Daisy's apartment is on fire. We're trapped."

The siren wails in the background, ringing through the

phoneline. I'm not surprised, as they're the closest fire station, but the relief that fills me, that familiar and trusted help is on the way, is palpable.

"We're coming. Stay alive, Reid. You hear me?"

"Save Daisy," is all I say before I disconnect, pocketing my phone and setting the bag on her bed. She's eyeing the window like she's considering opening it. "Don't open the window. Try to stay calm, stay low. Firetrucks are on their way."

Her shoulders fall, and all I want to do is hold her, comfort her. But not yet. I've got to keep my head, and succumbing to the need to hold her will not get the things done that need to be done before it's too late.

"Grab anything in here irreplaceable." I turn to her dresser drawers and fill the rest of the huge bag with handfuls of bras and panties. I need to focus, but I can't stop my eyes returning to her time and time again. She's on the brink of panicking but doing everything she can to keep it together.

For a split second, I see her as I did weeks ago when she was stuck holding the spewing water pipe above her head in the basement of her shop. She was brave in spite of her fear. She can do this.

"Hey." I squeeze her hand before taking her laptop and phone and closing up her bag. Finally, I hold her by her arms. "You're going to be okay. They'll be here before the fire makes it through the door."

Her gaze darts to the floor. "The shop."

"Its fireproof barrier will keep the fire at bay long enough to get out." I pray that's not a lie.

"But my apartment—"

I tighten my grip, garnering her eyes. "We don't know where it started or what's on fire. All I know is there's fire on the other side of that door, and there's no escape that way." I pull her into my chest.

"So, after all this, after last night. This is how we die?" she sobs.

Not if I can fucking help it.

I swipe at her tears before taking her mouth in what had better not be our last kiss. "No. This is *not* how you die." I fight to stay strong, keep my voice steady, offering her strength when all I feel is uncertainty.

Keep calm. Stay alive. Save her.

She gasps when she catches on to my word choice. "Not how *I* die? *I* die?"

Stay strong, baby.

I keep her near as we hunker on the floor on her side of the bed, closest to the window and farthest from the fire. I wet a couple of t-shirts I found in her closet, wrapping them around our heads and tying them in the back, covering our noses and mouths. "*We're* not dying."

I glance at the door, trying to time it just right, praying I'll hear sirens before I have to make a hard decision we may never come back from.

"Reid?"

Don't ask, Flower.

I hug her close. "I love you, my Wildflower."

Her sobs kill me as she seizes my shirt and cries into my neck.

Fate is a fickle fuck. Daisy is finally mine, and this is what happens?

"Is this where we die?"

"No," I whisper into her ear. *Please, no,* I pray.

The room is so hot, I'm dripping sweat, but maybe the moisture will only help us both. I've delayed as long as I dare. Smoke is seeping in; fire will be next. Holding her tight, I move to the window, unlocking it and sliding it up, pray the extra oxygen doesn't make the fire surge through her door.

Before she realizes what's happening, I carefully set her on the grate outside her window. My heart pounding, my hands shaking, I hold her a moment longer.

Keep calm. Stay alive. Save HER.

I cup her face, terrified to let go—never wanting to let go. "This is where you start the rest of your life."

"Reid?" Panic flashes in her eyes, and she starts to shake when she realizes where she is. The fresh air only highlights the smokiness of her room.

"Don't move, Daisy." I reach behind me, grabbing her bag and tossing it out the window. Locking on her shimmering pale green eyes, I give her the only truth I can, "I don't know how sturdy that grate is, but it should hold till the trucks get here."

"Reid?" She panics, her whole body trembling, shaking the false balcony.

It'll hold for just a few minutes for them to arrive. It has to.

"Don't move, baby." I release her, gripping the window, hating my next words as they rip up my throat like they're coated in glass. "I have to close the window to keep the fire at bay."

"No. Don't—"

"I love you, Daisy." My eyes burn as I lower the window, clenching my teeth, my entire body protesting the thought of leaving her—of dying without her.

"Reid, please," she begs, full on sobbing.

I lock it. Sealing her fate.

Perhaps sealing mine.

Save. Her.

"Reid!"

I press my hand to the window. "Don't move, baby," I rasp as tears fall. I slip from her view, resting my back against the wall next to the window, out of sight.

"Save her," I pray as I close my eyes and grip my hair.

"Reid!" she screams, breaking my heart and nearly my resolve, tempting me to pull her back in. But that's what a selfish man would do: hold on tight, dragging her down with me for my own comfort, only to get a few more precious moments with her before we both…

She has to live.

This is the *only* way.

CHAPTER 2

THE DOCTOR SAID I DIED. REID SET ME ON the ledge to survive. The rickety old building was giving away around us—him—as I prayed for the firetrucks to make it to us in time to save him.

Not me. *Him.*

My giant sequoia.

He said he loved me. Then left me. Alone. With orders of "Don't move."

He practically barked it.

Actually, he was quite tender about it. Break-my-heart tender.

Kind and gentle. That's my guy.

Was my guy?

I was…

Did I tell you I died?

I might still be dead. It's so dark. My brain, foggy. My thoughts, scattered. I'm not certain I'm living. I could be stuck in the in-between. Or hell is always a possibility.

He put me on the ledge and left me.

He. Left. Me.

And I died.

Buzzing and voices fill the room, my ears, but I can't make it out.

A name. My name. *I hear you!*

I can't move.

I can't scream.

I can't see!

It's dark. Too dark.

Reid. Why did you leave me?

Light flickers.

Dims.

Then brightness has me flinching and growling, "Stop."

"Ah, there she is." A tall, light-haired guy in a white lab coat flickers before me, too close, then becomes comfortable to look at as he eases back. His smile is soft and gentle. "Sorry, Ms. Webb. I was checking your pupils. We had a hard time waking you up from the anesthesia. I'm glad you're back with us."

Back? "Where am I?" I groan when I try to keep my eyes open and wince when I lift my arm to cover the light.

"Here." He turns off the piercing light over my head. "You're just coming out of surgery. I'm Doctor Moore, your anesthesiologist." He nods to the redhead working on a beeping machine. "This is Nurse Petra. She'll stay with you in recovery until you're ready to be moved to a room. Dr. Rankin will be in to see you shortly."

"Okay." I blink up at him. He's nice.

"Now that you're awake, feel free to rest." He chuckles.

Yeah, I'm thinking I don't have much of a choice. My eyelids feel like sandpaper and heavy like I have boulders for lashes.

The nice nurse gets the machine to stop beeping, keeping my head from splitting in two. Her gentle smile has me trying to smile back as she says, "There's somebody here who will be happy to know you're…"

If the nurse finishes her thoughts, I don't hear it. I don't hear anything other than the whooshing in my ears.

"Where is she?! I need to see her. Be sure she's okay!" I fight to get off the gurney, but the male nurse and Galant hold me down as though I'm some crazed civilian about to go crashing through the hospital, knocking doctors out of the way to find her. Though I'm tempted to—if I can just get up—I know they have a job to do, and so do I. I need to be sure my girl's okay, as she wasn't the last time I saw her.

She was having trouble…

She couldn't…

They took her from me before…

D.M. DAVIS

"Dammit, Reid. Calm the fuck down. She's still in surgery. You can't see her. Not yet, anyway. Let the doctor finish examining you before I knock you the fuck out myself," Galant barks, alleviating several of my concerns at once and eliminating my options—the operating room is off-limits, so there's nowhere for me to rush to... yet.

"Fine." I stop fighting and bite through the pain in my left ankle I'm quite sure I've fucked up irreparably.

"This is going to hurt." The doc eyes the nurse and my brother. "You got him?"

"What's going to hurt?" I scowl at the doctor.

"I need to examine your ankle. By the looks of it, it's fractured, maybe broken," Dr. Dick states as if I haven't taken years of first aid training and treated people when the paramedics are late.

That and the fact I *can feel* the damage shredding my patience.

But when I finally catch the visual state of my ankle and foot, the intent in the doctor's eyes, and the needle in the second nurse's hand, I reconsider. I should let them do their job. After all, I don't know where my Daisy is going to be taken for recovery. If she's just been taken into surgery as Galant advised, I have little hope of doing much before security runs me down. Plus, I'm not sure how useful I'll be to her on one good leg.

Receiving my own treatment while they're taking care of her only makes sense. There's no way I'd be lying here if she was anywhere I could reach her. I know myself well enough when it comes to her...

"Do it," I say to the doc but point at Nurse Needles. "I don't

22

need that." I narrow my eyes on Galant. "I don't want drugs. I need to stay sober—awake—for Daisy."

"Yeah, okay." Galant nods to the nurse and doctor. "He's trained and aware. He can take it, I vouch for him."

"I wouldn't recommend it. It's going to hurt like hell."

Nothing could hurt as badly as hearing my Wildflower falling from the grate outside her window as it broke and me being helpless to stop it—or break her fall with my body as a last resort.

I grab the sides of the bedframe, frustration rising faster than the pain. Every moment he spends warning me about pain is another wasted not getting on with it so I can be there waiting for my Daisy when she wakes up. "Do it!" I grit through clenched teeth.

"Hold him tight," Doc Dick instructs. He's making such a production out of this. It's not like he's resetting my leg. It's my fucking ankle, and there's no protruding bones that I can see.

"Ready?" Is he asking for me or himself? My confidence in his ability is now falling rapidly. He prods my ankle then tries to move my foot.

The roar that scrapes from the bowels of hell out of me shakes my entire body, if not the whole damn floor. Maybe not a fucking quick fix after all.

"We need an x-ray. There's no point in trying to manipulate it further if you need surgery, which I suspect you do. Unfortunately, Dr. Vasil, our orthopedic surgeon, won't be back for two days." He pops off his gloves. "We'll cross that bridge when we see what the x-rays reveal."

It's unbelievable how my concern for my Daisy blocked this level of pain. I focus on not passing out as he continues, "I'm starting you on antibiotics to stave off infection." He pierces me with his stern gaze. "I suggest you take the pain meds. You're going to need them. If not for you, for my staff's sake—and the other patients' eardrums." He gives further instructions to the nurses before fleeing the room.

"He's right." Galant gets in my line of sight. "You need to take the meds as directed so you can heal. You fuck up your ankle or foot, you can't be a fireman any longer."

My first instinct is to tell him to fuck off, but he's right. Only, the idea of not being a fireman isn't my concern. It's not being at 100% for Daisy, not being able to care for her. "After I see my girl."

He nods like he expected no other answer. "Alright."

Everyone seems to take a collective breath.

"Your room should be ready shortly." The male nurse checks his beeping phone, advising the person on the other line, "I'll be right there."

"I want a room with Daisy," I say to Galant and the nurses.

The nurse nods. "I'll see what I can do."

"You're going to be a pain in the ass, aren't you?" Galant's attention bounces from me to his phone as he texts.

"Not as long as I get what I need."

Galant squints at me. "And what's that?"

"To be with my Flower."

CHAPTER 3

THE ROAR OF THE BUILDING TUMBLING down around me, rubble hitting me, knocking the breath from my body, and fire licking at my skin have me screaming awake, slapping at my burning arms. Flames.

There are no flames.

I'm not on fire.

There's only shooting pain and the damn beeping of the monitor next to my bed at a rate that can't be right. I scan the room. Beige walls, beige blinds, speckled linoleum floor, wood doors, and an empty turquoise lounger are all that greet me.

The room is eerily quiet, except for the incessant beeping and my ragged inhales. I take a few cleansing breaths that hurt like hell and slump back against the raised head of the bed.

Hospital.

I'm not dead.

I'm in a hospital.

"Daisy!" seeps in from the hall amongst the low rumble of footfalls, shouting, and someone or something hitting the wall… repeatedly.

"Reid!" I cough, despite my throat not caring about my need to holler his name till he finds me. "Reid!" I try again.

I'm not dead.

He's not dead.

"Daisy, I'm coming!" He's closer.

"Sir, you can't—"

"Just watch me." My door flies open, and in tumbles my Sequoia. "Daisy," he pants, sweaty and out of breath.

I try to sit up, but the pain from my injuries—I'm not even sure what they are, or my state of being, other than knowing I'm not dead as previously thought—keeps me in place.

"You're alive," I whisper in awe. I heard his voice. *Knew* it was him. But until this moment, I didn't dare contemplate his fate beyond my own.

"Flower…" He reaches for me, hobbling on one leg.

"Dammit, Reid." His oldest brother stumbles through the door, followed by his other brother.

"Shit, you move fast for a guy with one working foot."

My eyes fly to Reid and down his body. He's in a hospital

gown, barefoot, and one leg is wrapped from knee to foot, bent and off the ground as he wobbles before me.

"Reid?"

"It's nothing. I'm fine." He makes one last hop and collapses in the turquoise chair beside my bed. "You—"

"Mr. Ashford, you're not supposed to be up." A male nurse rolls a wheelchair into the room. "Please sit in this, keep your leg elevated." He swipes at the sweat on his brow like he's been running after Reid for a while now. By the state of his brothers and Reid, it seems he gave quite a chase.

Was he running to me?

My heart thunders at the thought, the damn monitor beeping again. He was running *to me*. Tears loom as I reach for him.

He pulls his gaze off me to study the noisy machine before he glances at the nurse and the chair being wheeled over to him. "Fine," Reid grumbles, allowing the nurse and his brothers to get him into the wheelchair with little issue. Except when the nurse lifts his left leg onto the raised platform, Reid swears, grimacing through the pain, and starts to turn a little green.

"He's gonna puke." One of his brothers grabs the wash basin from the sink area and shoves it under Reid's chin.

Reid bats it away. "I don't need that." He sheepishly glances my way before stiffening his back to the room full of his brothers and two nurses. "Give us a moment."

He might not be his normal powerhouse self, but I don't think he's going to back down on this. I don't want him to. I'm anxious for his touch, to know he's really okay.

He left me on that ledge, that stupid fake balcony. And then I—

"I'll be back to check on you in a few minutes," his nurse advises, glancing between us.

"We'll be outside." His oldest brother pushes the other toward the door.

"Daisy, Dr. Rankin will be here in a bit to see you," my nurse advises.

I nod, but my focus is on Reid, who's trying to situate his chair closer but having trouble with his leg sticking out at a ninety-degree angle in front of him.

"Fuck it." He sits on the edge of my bed with more finesse than he should be capable of given his size and condition.

I don't mind the dip in the bed. I want him close. I want him next to me. "Your leg—"

"Is fine." He waves it off, taking my hand. "Daisy, fuck. I'm sorry."

"I thought—" I choke on a sob and retch in pain. *I thought I'd lost you.* "You left me," I manage on a wheeze.

He flinches at my words.

I didn't mean... I do—he left me—but... "I thought I lost you." The monitor starts beeping again.

"Breathe—" Worry coats his demeanor as he checks the monitor and the thing on my finger. He squeezes my hand. "Try to relax and breathe, Flower."

I'm trying.

He's here. I'm alive.

He's alive.

28

He's here.

My nurse rushes through the door. "Oxygen!" She slaps a mask on my face, covering my nose and mouth. "Try to calm down. Breathe, Daisy. That's it." Her stern brow turns on Reid. "If you're going to upset her, you need to leave. You should be in your own bed anyway."

"I'm not leaving her," he growls.

I try to suck in air as she continues to chastise him, "You can bark at me all you want, Mr. Ashford, but you will leave if you put her life in danger. She just had major surgery. She had a metal rod removed from her back and a collapsed lung repair, not to mention the broken ribs and head laceration from her fall."

"I know." Reid grips my hand, his eyes pleading with me. "I was there."

"Rei—"

"Don't try to talk." He brushes my cheek. "Just breathe." He switches from tender to grump depending on whom he's looking at or speaking to. Thankfully, I get the tender version.

I squeeze his hand to garner his eyes. His brow rises, and I point to his leg, not speaking, as he requested.

"It's my ankle. I'm fine." He kisses our joined hands. "I'll be fine." He brushes at my tears. "It's you I'm worried about."

"You'll be fine once you get back in bed and get your foot up. You need surgery too." Nurse Petra is not messing around.

"I'll heal better knowing she's okay." His eyes mist over as he studies me like he can heal me from sheer determination alone.

"She'll be fine. She just needs rest." With that the nurse steps back. "Don't take the mask off. Once your numbers are better, we'll wean you off." She gives him a pointed glare before leaving.

He presses his lips to my brow. "I'm sorry—" he starts but stops when the door opens again, and Mary walks in.

I frown when her gaze bounces between me and Reid. She finally lands on me. "Daisy, I'm so glad you're okay." She moves closer. "Or will be. You need anything—"

"I got her, Mom."

I'm sorry, what?!

"You should be in your own bed." She's angry as she takes in our closeness. "You could have told me, you know."

"Mom, please. Not now." His uneasy gaze flicks to me.

"Mary is your mom?" I finally manage, though my reply is muffled by the mask.

Neither of them answers. They're too busy glaring at each other.

Frustrated, I pull off the oxygen mask. "You're his mom?"

Her head pops to me. "Yes—"

"I can explain," Reid interjects.

I frown, trying to understand. He's been coming into my flower shop to see me every Tuesday for over a year. Mary has been trying to get me to agree to a blind date with her son for ages. They're...

"Did you know I knew your mom?" Anger rises, numbing the pain in my body. "Was this a game?" I push his hand away. "See who could get me to say yes first?"

Mary blanches. "Daisy, it's not—"

30

"It's not like that," Reid tries again, panic riddling his pain-streaked face.

"I can't…" I tear at the sheets, trying to fill my lungs.

Beeping is all I hear as my eyes roll back and I arch, lungs burning, a ten-ton weight on my chest.

"Daisy!"

CHAPTER 4

"OUT! OUT! OUT!" HER NURSE ORDERS AS she rushes to my girl.

"Daisy!" I'm not leaving. "I'm so sorry. Breathe, baby. Please breathe."

"Oh god," Mom gasps.

"Reid, you need to give them room to help Daisy." Galant and Turner start to pull me from the room when I refuse to get in the wheelchair.

"No! I'm not leaving her!" Never. Never leaving her again.

She thinks I left her.

She thinks our love was a game.

My mom pinches my chin, leaning in close. "Do you want to kill her?!"

I freeze. What? "No, of course not." I glance back to my Flower as one nurse pushes IV meds while the other checks her vitals. "I can't leave—"

"You can. You are." Mom directs my brothers to continue dragging me out of her room and down the hall.

Once I stop fighting, they lower me into the wheelchair my mom was pushing after us.

"You care for her, Reid. I know you do—"

"I love her. She loves me." Or she *did* before I put her on that ledge believing I abandoned her. She doesn't understand it was the hardest thing I've ever done. Leaving her so she could survive.

Mom nods, concern marring her normally cheery demeanor. "Good. That's good. But she's had a horrible shock on top of surgery and nearly dying—"

Don't remind me. The thought of losing her has my need to protect raring up, willing to fight them all over again.

"—she needs time to heal, to process the knowledge that we know each other. We didn't intentionally betray her by not being open about our connection to each other and her, but we weren't forthcoming either. To some, that feels the same."

"She can be mad at me while I'm standing right in front of her." *Keeping her safe.*

"You can't stand—" Turner starts.

"Shut it," Galant cuts him off, clasping my shoulder before rounding my wheelchair to get in my face. "She's having trouble breathing, man. You're causing her stress. She's not *mad*. She's trying to *survive* in there." He motions down the hall where her room is. "Give her time to deal with her injuries, then you can be all stubborn and insist she take her anger and frustration out on you, but right now, she can barely breathe." His last words are so soft, as if it pains him to admit it.

"Fuck." He's right. I'm being selfish. I want to be in there for her, but also for me. I need her probably more than she needs me right now.

I guess time will tell. "Take me back to my room. I'm ready for those pain pills."

If I can't be with her, numbing my body from the pain might make it bearable.

Barely.

Three days later, my body full of more drugs than I care for, the orthopedic surgeon is back from vacation to operate on my ankle, which is fractured and requires hardware for stability. Galant and Turner have taken turns keeping my miserable ass company as I grumble and sleep the days away.

My thoughts are never far from Daisy. I'm not family, so I can't get updates. She refuses to see Mom or my brothers. I've contemplated sending Theo in to see if she can break through the emotional barrier my Flower has erected. Though, my sister isn't much better at being patient than I am, so I'm not sure her tactics would be any more successful than mine.

Because of Daisy's breathing issues, she can't have any

flowers, though I doubt she's allergic to anything, given her line of work. It also seems insensitive to send her flowers when she just lost her beloved flower business.

No one else's bouquets would be as nice as hers would have been. It's ironic.

Daisy needs an apology, yet I can't give one if she won't see me, return my calls or texts.

She's incommunicado.

The silence is killing me one millisecond at a time.

I say my farewells to my family and pray they wheel my bed past Daisy's room for one last stolen glance.

No such luck.

Before I can protest or ask for the hundredth time how she is, they push drugs into my IV to knock me out.

Maybe when I wake up, she'll be sitting next to me, checking on me, wondering how I am instead of me worrying over her. Missing her.

"He looks so peaceful," I whisper to Galant. "You sure he's fine?" I swipe at my tears that don't seem to stop these days.

"Yeah, Doc said everything looks good. He just has to stay the course, and he should heal right as rain."

I frown. "Is rain right?"

He chuckles through a shrug. "I don't even know what many of the stupid colloquialisms I say mean."

"Same."

"He's worried about you."

"I know."

"Will you wait to talk to him?"

I can't. "No." I slowly back away toward the curtain that sections off his recovery bed from all the others.

I want to touch him, hold his hand, kiss his quiet, pouty mouth. Which means I need to leave before I lose my nerve to leave at all. I can't chance waking him, giving him hope when there is none by letting him see me standing vigil.

"Where will you go?"

"Home." I say it like it means something. It doesn't.

Galant nods like he knows where home is. *I* don't even know where that is anymore. All my worldly belongings, except my car and the bag Reid haphazardly packed for me, burned up in the fire. All I have is that bag and the clothes Mary was kind enough to bring me. She didn't force a conversation. She simply slipped inside my room, leaving the bag with fresh clothes, my laptop and phone. She must have added in the shoes and toiletries as none of that was packed, and the brands are unfamiliar.

I don't even smell like myself. A small loss but it feels heavier, signifying another part of me burned, destroyed, gone. But I'm still here because of...

"Will you be back?" Galant's sorrowful brown eyes, so much like Reid's, tug on my heartstrings.

"I don't know." I lost everything here. I could rebuild or start fresh somewhere less... Reid-centric. He's impacted every part of my life for more than a year. He's in the air, under my skin, stealing my thoughts, ripping out my heart.

I swipe at another tear and take one more look at my Sequoia before turning to slip out of his recovery bay and out of his life, this town for now—maybe forever.

"He's sorry," Galant's quiet plea makes me still, my back to them both.

"Me too." Reid felt like my *forever*. Now I don't know what was truth and what was a lie—a game to him and his mom, maybe even his family.

"What do I tell him when he wakes up?"

I glance over my shoulder, ignoring his flinch when he catches my tears freefalling without reprieve. "Tell him…" *I love him. I never want to be without him.* "Goodbye."

"I can't tell him that. He'll rip this place apart trying to find you." He steps closer, gripping my arm, not hard, but firm enough to emphasize the worry in his eyes.

Yeah, Reid just might tear this place apart based on how he reacted when they *tried* to keep him from me the night of the fire.

I turn completely, surprising Galant with a hug, ignoring the pain in my ribs and shoulder. "Tell him if he calls, I'll answer if I can. If he texts, I reply when I'm able." I pull back, catching Galant's faint smile. "Tell him… I need time." *And that I love him.*

I love him

I love him…

He nods. "*That* I can do." He reaches into his pocket and holds out a wad of cash.

I frown at his hand, leaning away. "What's that?"

"It's from the guys at the firehouse. We know you lost

everything, even your purse, ID, credit cards. It'll help you get where you're going."

I shouldn't take it, but he's right. I don't have a penny on me. Banks are already closed, and I don't have any ID to prove I am who I say I am when they reopen in the morning. Another problem I'll have to figure out when I get to my dad's. "Thank you. I'll pay you back."

"No need. Just do me one favor."

"Yeah, okay."

"When he calls—which will be sooner than later—don't kill his hope."

"I don't know—"

"You don't have to *know* anything. He's hurting too. You need time. *He* needs time, but that doesn't mean you can't talk *while* you're taking that time."

"I can't argue with that." I could, but I don't want to. The idea of never talking to him again is inconceivable no matter how hurt or confused I am.

Time.

It could make or break us.

CHAPTER 5

I FLINCH AT THE BRIGHTNESS OF THE GLARING sun. It might be after five, but the big orange ball in the sky doesn't seem to know that or doesn't care. I catch sight of a car that looks like mine idling at the curb seconds before Turner opens the driver's door and steps out. "Your chariot awaits." He bows, motioning me forward.

"What did you do?"

He takes my bag and opens the back door. "I had it cleaned, tuned, and fueled." He sets my duffel on the back seat and closes the door. "Had to be sure it was safe for you to drive to…" He quirks a brow, waiting on me to fill in the blank.

"My dad's." It's not exactly what he's after. "And the keys?"

"No big deal to get replacements when you know who to ask." His grin is mischievous and nearly makes me laugh, but I'm too close to crying again over his and Galant's kindness.

I wish I'd taken the time to get to know them better *before* all of this happened. They're just as caring and protective as Reid is, even though I'm the one leaving their brother.

"Tell your mom goodbye for me."

His surprise has him stilling for a second. "She'll be happy to know you thought of her, but not happy to hear *goodbye*."

She hurt me, but not enough for me to be rude or not acknowledge the kindness and space she's given me to work through it all. Not that I know how I feel about it. Honestly, the only thing I know is I love him, but I'm deeply hurt. The betrayal won't let me sit around and be overcome by his voice, his size, his ability to knock me stupid with a single heated gaze. He saved me, but if the fire hadn't happened and I'd found this out, I'd still need time and a whole bunch of space.

I'm grateful, but gratitude can't be the reason we're together. With a final thanks, I drive away.

My future is uncertain, my destiny is not. Dad has an above-garage apartment at his place near the beach. He said it's mine for as long as I need it, even offered me a job I'm not in any position to turn down. Until the insurance money comes in, I'll be living off my savings, which is not small but not near enough to start over. I need to save as much as I can.

My surgeon gave me a local doctor who will handle my post-op care. But before too much reality takes over, I need a few days to relax and heal. I can't wait to get lost in the sand and sun, soaking it up, breathing in the salty air, and just… be.

"Flower?" I smell her. She's close. Opening my eyes, I blink a few times and frown when it's Galant's stern mug staring down at me.

"Happy to see you too, man." He smiles. Don't see that too often. He's the grump in the family. "How you feelin'?"

"Woozy." I scan the curtained-off area. I guess I'm in recovery. I survived surgery. Now, if I can just survive missing my Wildflower. "She here?"

He doesn't even pretend not to know who I'm talking about. "No." He looks like he has more to say, but he stays silent. Typical.

I guess I should be grateful he's not rubbing it in my face. Though, that's more Turner's MO.

"How'd the surgery go?" If he won't talk about Daisy, maybe he'll tell me how soon I can get out of here and find her.

"Good. Doc said it went as planned. No surprises." He leans in. "You need to follow instructions and not push your healing. He says the worst thing you can do is put weight on your foot too soon and screw up all his hard work."

"'Cause it's all about him, right?" I chuckle and groan. I'm still sore as fuck from the fall from her window. Lying in bed for days at a time hasn't helped.

"No, smartass. It's about letting your ankle heal so you can walk again without a limp, and getting back to firefighting where we need you. Walk too soon and it could heal wrong. You could do permanent damage, Reid. This is serious."

"I got it. Don't try to use my foot until the doctor says I can."

He falls into the seat next to the bed. "I'll remind you of that when you're trying to get up and go to Daisy."

"I can wheel myself down the hall." I'm not too weak to do that.

"It won't matter."

"What? Why?"

"She checked herself out. She's gone."

The fuck. "You just let her leave?! Where'd she go?!" My voice gets louder with each word.

His hand hits my chest seconds before a nurse comes running in. "Mr. Ashford, do I need to sedate you?"

"No. Fuck. I just woke up. I found out my girl is gone. Give me a goddamn minute to process it."

She flinches and steps back.

Fuck. "Sorry. I—" I wave my hand. "Need a second, okay?"

She nods and smiles softly. "You should be ready to move back to your room now that you're awake."

"Great," I grit through my teeth, trying not to be a total dickwad.

"I'll check on you in a few, as soon as I finish up with another patient." She slips out quietly.

I turn my attention to Galant.

He sits back down, trusting I won't throw myself out of the bed and drag my body to wherever the fuck she went. I don't plan on it, but I'm not making any promises.

"She was here," he confirms.

I did smell her. I wasn't imagining it. That makes me feel significantly less out of touch with reality—tough with the pain meds still causing a haze. "When?"

"While you were still conked out. She still cares but needs time. She said you can call her, text her, and she'll respond when she can. It's progress, right?"

Maybe. "You really don't know where she went?"

"She would only say she's going to her dad's."

"When's she coming back?"

He just stares.

"She's not coming back?" Panic surges. Taking time to cool off is one thing; completely ghosting me is another.

"She doesn't know. I think you have everything to do with whether she does or not. So, you need to stay calm and get your head on straight. Decide what you want and make every decision based on that. Don't let your ego short-circuit your long-term goal."

I relax into the bed. He's making sense. He usually does. "Wake me up when it's time to leave." When it's time to get my girl. Or, at least, a few hours before.

I'm making contact as soon as I'm back to my room and my cell phone. I'll text her, ease into the idea of talking to me, show her she means everything to me. It wasn't a game... even if she can't see that right now. If I jump into a phone call first thing, I'll either beg her to come back or get pissy when she says she can't.

She needs time. I understand.

So do I. Time to make a plan to win her back.

CHAPTER 6

I T'S LATE WHEN I PULL INTO MY DAD'S driveway and continue around the side of the house to the detached garage. The house has an *attached* two-car garage, but Dad can never have enough garage or workshop space for his babies: his cars, motorcycles, surfboards and gear. He built the additional garage years ago with an apartment above, where I'll be staying.

The place is dark except for the exterior lights that switch on upon my arrival. I might think he was sleeping if I didn't know better. He texted hours ago, letting me know he'd be out late and the hide-a-key was in the same old spot. He said to make myself at home, and that he'd put food in the apartment fridge. Knowing my dad, that could mean it's stocked with fresh veggies and fruit, or day-old pizza boxes, depending on where he is in his heathy eating journey.

I ate on the road anyway, so tonight, it doesn't really matter. All I want is a glass of ice water, a shower, and bed. In that order. My entire body hurts. Driving on the highway wasn't bad, but turning the steering wheel with a bum shoulder and cracked ribs is for the birds.

I checked myself out of the hospital early, against doctor's orders. I just couldn't stand to stay in that room alone for one more day. The silence, the loneliness, the sadness wrapping around me, nearly strangling me. The doctor was going to let me go in a few days anyway. I promised to take it easy—and I intend to. Just as soon as I make it up the stairs.

I step out into the cool night air, and the sea breeze is exactly what I need. I can't wait to see the view in the morning. Sunrise—or sunset—on the beach can't be beat. Grabbing my bag with my good arm, again ignoring my body's protests, I find the spare key and trek up the stairs—slowly. I'm so winded by the top, I have to sit on the last step to catch my breath. I know my body needs time to heal, but damn, it's discouraging how weak I am. I may need more than a few days before I'm ready to work at Rob's Surf Shop.

"You need a hand?" The deep timbre at the bottom of the stairs reminds me of one man, but he's not here.

My eyes land on Sage, my younger brother. "Hey. I didn't know you'd be here." Dad didn't mention it, but then again, he's not big on details or being home to greet his daughter he hasn't seen in two years.

"I was waiting for you." Sage climbs to me.

"You were?" I have to lean back to take all of him in. When did he grow so tall?

His smile is knowing. "Yeah, I'm not Dad, remember?"

Yeah, and I'm not like Mom. I don't know where we got our sense of family, but it wasn't from our wandering parents. I guess Dad has laid down roots. He's just not one to be tied down by commitment other than his surf shop.

Sage offers his hand, helping me up. "I fell asleep, so it took me a minute to realize you were here." He takes my bag, following me to the door. "You're hurtin', huh?"

"Yeah, a metal rod through my lung took the wind out of my get-up-and-go."

"Ouch." He kisses my head as he passes me, opening windows and turning on lights as he goes. "There're fresh sheets on the bed. I stocked the fridge with your favorites, but if there's something you need, just let me know."

He did all that. Figures Dad would take credit.

Sage draws near, pulling me into a gentle hug. "I'm sorry you're hurt. Give it time. You're the toughest girl I know. You'll be right as rain in no time."

There's that saying again. Does it mean something?

"Thanks. I just want a shower and bed for now. But I appreciate it."

He steps back, running his long fingers through his curly sun-bleached hair. "I'll stop by with breakfast in the morning. I've got a key, if you're okay with me letting myself in in case you're still sleeping."

"Yeah—" I kiss his cheek, "that'd be great. I may sleep till dinnertime, though."

He chuckles. "I'll just check to be sure you're breathing."

"Tell Dad not to expect me at the shop for a few days."

"I told him it'd be at least a week and then only part-time." His pale green eyes match mine but seem wiser than the last time I saw him.

"When did you grow up?" It's meant to be wistful but actually hurts knowing it happened without me around.

"While you were gone," he confirms.

"Sorry."

"Nope. No apologies. You babied me. I needed to grow up. Now, I can baby you while you're healing." He smiles on a nod as he opens the door. "Call if you need something. No matter the time."

"Thanks," my voice cracks.

"It's good to have you home, no matter the circumstances."

He's gone before I can reply.

I close and lock the door, shuffle to the kitchen for that long drink of ice water, then strip on my way to the shower. The heat of the water scorches then soothes as it runs along my body, seeping in, easing my aches and pains.

After my shower, I'm feeling slightly better and take time to put the few belongings I have away in the closet or dresser. One thing I don't have is a charger for my phone—I forgot to grab it in the chaos of the fire. I'll have to buy one tomorrow—or ask

Sage to do it. He seems amenable to the idea of helping me out despite me not being around as much as I should have been.

It'll be nice to spend this time with him, working alongside him at the surf shop. Though, I'm sure he'll be busy with lessons most of the summer. Still, it's been years. He was away at college when I moved to open my shop. I could have done it here, but I wanted to find my own way out of the shadow of my dad and his bigger-than-life reputation. Some people call him a surf bum. Most think of him as a god, one of the most talented surfers to surf these shores or the world at large. People either want to be him, friend him, or sleep with him. I don't need or want to be in the middle of all that. But here I am. Right back in the thick of it.

I didn't have much of a choice.

Reid would say otherwise, I'm sure.

Reid. How is he?

I climb in bed and grab my phone from the nightstand. I take a few deep breaths, working through the pain before checking to see if he texted or called.

As much as I feel betrayed, I'm torn between elation and dread when I see missed texts from him. He didn't call, though. I thought for sure that would be his first choice. Or maybe that's just me wishing for a voicemail so I could hear his voice while having space. Selfish, but…

Reid: *Surgery went well. I should be up and about in no time.*

Reid: *I hope you make it to your father's without incident.*

Then an hour or so later.

Reid: *You left without a goodbye.*

Reid: *Let me know you're safe. Please.*

The latter texts are more what I anticipated. The first two are way more platonic and civil than I would expect from my fiery Sequoia.

I don't know what to say but decide honesty is the best course.

Me: *I'm safely at my dad's. Glad your surgery went well. Praying for a full recovery.*

Damn, now I sound cold and entirely too professionally cordial. I try again.

Me: *I miss you. I'm hurt. I need time.*

Dots start bouncing immediately as if he was waiting for me to open my heart to him, baffled by my first attempt at civility. *Yeah, me too.*

Reid: *I'm sorry for hurting you. Take what you need.*

Take what I need? Hmm, it's so much. But right now...

Me: *I need sleep. Good night.*

Reid: *Night, Flower.*

CHAPTER 7

WITH ALL THE DRUGS I'VE BEEN ON, YOU'D think I'd have no trouble sleeping. Sadly, that's not the case. But this time, it's not my restlessness that wakes me.

Ringing pulls me from a fitful sleep.It takes a second to figure out it's my phone and not my IV machine or some other hospital contraption down the hall.

I thought my heart couldn't beat much faster from jerking awake. I was wrong. When I see who's calling and the time, if I had a heart monitor, it would be going off right about now.

"Daisy?"

"Reid," my girl sobs.

"What's wrong?" I sit up, raising my bed to meet my back, contemplating how fast I can get out of here. Can I drive like this? If she needs me, I'm going to be laying on that horn the entire way, other drivers beware.

"You're okay?"

Am I okay? I still, squelching my escape plans—for now. "What happened, baby? It's nearly three in the morning. You should be sound asleep."

"I was—" She sucks in a stunted breath. "I keep having dreams about the fire. Me. You. Dying."

"I'm fine—"

"I needed to hear your voice… to be sure."

"I'm right here, Flower. I'm not leaving you, and you're fine."

She cares. She called to check on me.

I lower my bed and settle in for a chat with *my* girl. She needed to hear my voice. That matters, even if we're just starting the road to recovery together—but apart.

"How's your dad?"

"My… Oh, he's fine. I mean, I haven't seen him, but I'm sure he's fine. I saw my brother Sage, though."

"Wait. You drove all the way to stay with your father, and he's not there?" WTF? Who's going to watch out for her, help her if she needs it? Carry her fucking bag I know she shouldn't be lifting this soon after surgery.

"He's in town. He was just out when I arrived. Sage helped me get inside."

There are so many things wrong with that sentence. "Helped you inside?"

"I'm still pretty weak. Climbing the stairs to the garage apartment were harder than I anticipated."

The rickety old iron staircase to the apartment over her shop is what I envision. Then the idea of her falling and no one there to help her—especially not her father—has me fuming for her and sad for us.

She left me for that?

She must really be pissed.

But she's called me...

"I came to see you before I left."

I knew that, but it means something, her admitting it.

"You were still out from your surgery. But I did see you even if you didn't know it."

As soon as I woke up, I sensed it on some level beyond the scent she left behind. "I wish you would have stayed."

Silence. I almost think she's hung up before she says, "I couldn't. It would've been too hard."

"I would have tried to convince you to stay."

"Which is exactly why I had to go."

I don't like her answer. I understand it. But I don't like it. "When did your nightmares start?"

"I woke up from surgery having one, or *something*. It might have been a memory. I'm not sure. What happened after you put me on the fake balcony is a little fuzzy."

"Daisy, I—"

"Please don't. Don't apologize. I'm not in a place to hear it, never mind accept it, and the idea of not forgiving you is too hard—"

"Okay. Please don't cry, baby." The sorrow in her voice is too much. "Tell me something you love about being at your father's."

"The ocean." The smile in her voice brings one to my lips as she continues, "The sun on my face and the sea breeze. There's a shack down the beach that has the best seafood boils around. I can't wait to eat there."

…with me? I want to experience all that with her. I want to walk on the beach hand in hand, but as I look down at my leg in traction, it obviously won't be for a while yet.

She needs time to heal. So do I.

"I'm going to text you every day." I want to call her, but I can already tell this tenuous connection—hearing her voice, her emotions—will be too much. And as soon as I'm able, I'll drive to find her, wherever she is. I know she's on the coast still, but closer to the beaches instead of rocky terrain where I am in Round Rock— where she *used* to live.

Texting is safer. Manageable.

But… if she calls. I'll answer.

"O-okay." Her disappointed tone gives me hope for us.

"You said you need time, Flower. The only way I can do that is to keep a connection with you, but hearing you hurting over the phone—in your voice instead of seeing words on a screen— it's too much. You want space, and I want to give it to you. The only way I can do that is to not hear your voice front and center reminding me of all the ways I could jump in and help. Of all the ways I miss you. Of all the ways I hurt you."

"I hate that."

"Me too."

53

I sigh in relief as she agrees, "Okay. I'll answer your texts."

"If you have a nightmare, you can call me—"

"No, it's okay, if my voice is too much, I—"

"If you need *me*, Wildflower, I'm there." I sigh, keeping a tight rein on my need to protect and comfort her. "Take what you need. It's yours, fully, when you're ready."

"I… Yeah, okay…"

I wish she would complete that thought. *I love you* is on the tip of my tongue. Was it on hers? "Get some sleep, Daisy."

"I'm sorry I woke you."

"I'm not." Not for a second.

She hums a sigh, "I'll *text* you later."

"Yeah, baby. Text you later."

I disconnect, staring at my phone for the longest time, feeling a peace I didn't think I could feel until she was back in my life, in my arms, forgiving me.

Soon.

I shoot off a text. Then put my phone on the hospital tray and get back to the business of healing.

I've got a girl to win back.

But first, I've got a body to heal.

The jiggle of the lock has me popping up in bed.

"Daisy?"

"Dad?" I rub my eyes, pulling the covers higher before he enters my bedroom.

He runs his fingers through his dirty-blond hair dusted with gray, only for it to flop back into his eyes, curls bouncing. His tall, athletic frame, graceful from years of surfing, stops a foot from my bed. He smiles, sun-worn laugh lines accentuating his blue gaze. He's still handsome. Sun-ripe and aged by the sea—he wouldn't have it any other way.

"Hey, sorry to wake you. I was hoping we could have breakfast together before I head out."

"I... uh, sure—" I catch the time on the clock next to my phone: 6:07. "Jeez, it's so early."

"You used to be an early bird."

I yawn and slowly turn to lower my feet to the side of the bed. "Yeah, well, I haven't been sleeping all that great—" *I used to have a reason to get up early...* I wince as my shoulder and ribs protest my movement. It'll get better if I can just get up and get moving.

He doesn't miss it. "You need help?"

I wave him off. "Give me ten, and I'll be downstairs."

He frowns, getting a good look at me. "Sage said you were in a bad way. You take all the time you need in healing, and it's okay if you don't feel up to coming down."

"No, I'd like to have breakfast with you guys."

"Good." He nods. "That's good." He turns to leave. "See you in a few." He hesitates at the door.

"I'm okay, Dad. I got this."

He lets out a breath. "Holler if you need help."

I wait until the apartment door closes before getting up. I don't want him to hear me groaning like an old woman.

It takes me a little longer than stated to do my business and dress. Sweat beads on my brow, making me rest between pulling on a t-shirt and shorts, huffing like I ran a mile. I fight tears and the ache in my throat, knowing this is exactly how Reid would have helped me: gently slipping my shirt over my head, tenderly guiding my arms through the holes, on bended knee helping me step into my shorts before he pulled them up over my hips, buttoning and zipping them up, a warm kiss to my brow. He would have loaded my toothbrush, set my shoes before me to slip on, held my hand as I braved the stairs.

I don't feel brave or smart for leaving him. I feel lonely and broken.

I do make it downstairs, moving about as fast as a tortoise, and enter the kitchen through the back door of Dad's cottage-style house.

Sage's eyes find me first. "Morning. You okay?" He frowns, taking in my stiffness as I slowly make my way to the table.

"Um, yeah, about as good as I can be, I guess." Is it too soon to change my mind, to drive home even though I have no home to go to?

He chuckles, lifting the coffee pot. "You still don't like coffee?"

"Actually, I'll have a cup with cream and sugar, please." I can't muster the desire to drink, much less make a smoothie. It was my thing with Reid, our special moment to bond over the concoctions I made, knowing he'd come in on Tuesdays to taste whatever flavor I dreamed up that morning—just for him.

Another thing lost, another piece of myself left behind.

Sage places a steaming cup in front of me just as I sit in a chair at the kitchen table. "Here's some vanilla creamer. You might like it more with that."

Sounds yummy. "Thanks."

"You still like your eggs over easy?" Dad asks from the stove.

"Yep." I drop in a sugar cube and fill my cup with as much creamer as it can take before it's near overflowing. Stirring slowly, my gaze slips out the kitchen window, catching sight of the morning waves breaking about a hundred feet from the water's edge. There's a shallow ledge that ends right where the waves break, which makes this place great for swimmers and sunbathers but not great for catching waves. Dad's shop is farther down, just past Dana Point where it's prime surfing.

I used to love to get up with them and go surfing. I'm not sure when it stopped being fun for me. Maybe around the time my parents split, Mom moved away, and Dad decided chasing tail was more interesting than raising the kids he had full custody of.

If I have any chance of enjoying my time here, I either have to forgive or let it go. The only person being hurt by my hurt is me. Dad is Dad. If he didn't or couldn't change for Mom, I doubt he'll change for me—or Sage. He has his moments, like now—he's here.

If I can forgive Dad, does that stand true for Reid and Mary? Was I right to leave? Or am I just pouting, licking my wounds?

I take a sip of coffee, focusing on the rich, sweetly bitter concoction instead of the state of my life, as it slips over my tastebuds, down my throat, and into my bloodstream.

When breakfast is over, I watch the boys drive off before climbing the stairs. It's easier than it was yesterday. That's progress.

But it's harder going up than it was coming down. I wonder if I could get one of those chairs that carry me up the stairs, like old rich people have in movies. I'd laugh at the thought if it wouldn't hurt so bad.

One step at a time.

But first, I'm going back to bed. It's only seven, and it's already been a long-ass day.

CHAPTER 8

I T'S BEEN TWO WEEKS OF HEALING AND steadily starting to feel a little more like my old self, physically at least. Emotionally, I'm a wreck. I miss Reid. I miss my store and my employees. I even miss Mary and bonding over flowers each week, but I'm not sure what that means for Reid and me. This is about me, not us.

I miss the routine.

I miss my bed. My stupid bed and pillows—all the things in my apartment that never mattered before.

The things I worked hard to be able to afford. It wasn't much, but it was *mine*.

It's been two weeks of texts from Reid, talking about everyday mundane stuff. There are no grand gestures.

No begging for forgiveness—though I did ask him not to ask—I'm not ready.

No asking me to come back to him either.

No talk of feelings other than how we're *physically* feeling.

I wasn't ready for him to act, but it feels a little like he's given up on being more than friends.

And that's just pouring salt into my open wounds. I came here to mend, to get my head on straight, to figure out my future. Yet all I feel is his heartbreaking absence and my festering emotional injuries.

I start part-time at Dad's surf shop next week. In the meantime, I've been keeping myself busy with sleeping an inordinate amount of time, reading, watching TV with Sage when he's home, and painting—mainly with oils. *That* I've really enjoyed. It's been years since I've painted anything that wasn't a vase for a flower arrangement. I was worried I'd lost the ability to paint on canvas. It's been far too long. It only took me a few days to feel at home in my skin while doing it. At first, it was undeniably awkward and forced.

Now, I lose hours. I'm working on a landscape at the moment—the ocean view from the apartment's living room window. Though it's not a good surfing spot, I've taken creative license in exaggerating the waves and added a surfer. His size and build look remarkably like my Sequoia. It was unintentional but not an unwelcomed detail.

I wonder if he surfs.

I decide to ask. There's nothing in our agreement that says I can't initiate communication.

Me: *Do you surf?*

I clean my brushes and put away my painting supplies for the day, not waiting to see if he replies. He could be sleeping.

When I'm done, I can't resist checking to see if the text even shows as read. To my surprise, he responded.

Reid: *No. Will you teach me?*

I'm shocked he admitted he doesn't. I figured he must have tried it at least a time or two growing up close to the California coast, granted Round Rock isn't right on the cliff line, but it's only an hour away. I never looked into it, but I'm sure Dad or Sage could tell me the nearest amazing surf spot only the locals know.

Not that it matters right now.

Me: *I'm afraid neither of us is in any shape to even try, ATM. But maybe—in the future—I could be persuaded.*

Reid: *That's not a no.*

No, surprisingly, it's not.

Reid: *I know we're not talking-talking, but you have to know…*

Reid: *I love you.*

Reid: *I don't intend on letting you slip away.*

He went there. I asked him not to, and he did it anyway. I can't help the flutters my heart is dancing to. Maybe it's a happy dance. Maybe a nervous one.

Me: *Reid*

Reid: *Wildflower*

Reid: *I'll do whatever it takes.*

Whatever it takes. I have no idea what it'll take…

Reid: *Even if it's not talking about forgiveness or love. Or how much I miss you.*

Me: *That's not fair.*

Is it? I've been feeling the disconnect. Him separating himself from the emotions of our relationship. And it hurt. Now he's offering up his heart—his truth… and it hurts like hell.

I hurt without it.

I hurt with it.

If it hurts no matter what, how will I ever know what I'm supposed to do?

Hurt with him—or hurt without him?

Reid: *I know. I just had to be sure you didn't forget. Be mad but don't doubt my love still burns for you.*

Me: *I thought you were a man of few words.*

Reid: *For you, I'm bursting with them.*

Me: *I miss you.*

Is it fair to say it? I don't know, but he's being open and vulnerable. It's only right I give him a little in return.

Reid: *Am I a dick to say I'm glad? There's a way to fix that. When you're ready.*

Me: *No, it's nice to be missed.*

Reid: *You say the word.*

Me: *What word?*

Reid: *OhmyholyGrandmaJean*

My breath catches. He remembers. He listens. He sees. He's being funny but through my laugh, I kinda want to cry too.

Me: *LOL. I should have guessed.*

Reid: *You're cute as fuck when you say it.*

Me: *Good to know.*

Reid: *Actually, you're beautiful all the time.*

Me: *Reid*

Reid: *Flower*

Reid: *I love your warnings. I love hearing my name on your lips. Soon, baby.*

Reid: *Damn, I have to go. Turner is here to pick me up for a family dinner.*

Family dinner. I haven't had one of those in… ever. Even as a little kid, it was usually Sage and I eating at the kitchen table alone. Our parents going out to eat or eating later or maybe not at all. I really don't remember. I just know it was only the rare holiday when we'd all sit at the dining room table together. It always felt awkward and fake.

Me: *Enjoy. Tell everyone hi.*

Reid: *I will. Take what you need, Flower.*

And what if it's you?

What if it's not you?

The thought brings tears to my eyes. I set my phone aside and turn on the TV.

While he's with his family, I'll be here alone, heating up left-overs or ordering Chinese.

I don't have any right to feel sorry for myself. Coming here was my choice.

Take what you need.

I should be flying high as Turner drives to our parents' house. She said she missed me and only slightly chastised me for saying I still love her.

"She didn't say it back," I mutter to the ether.

"What?"

Shit, I didn't think he heard me. "I told Daisy I love her. She didn't say it back."

He frowns. "When? Before the accident or now?"

"Today. We were texting."

"You still doing the not-talking-to-her thing?"

"Yeah, I can't bide my time if I hear the emotion in her voice." Or worse, *don't* hear it because she no longer cares.

"She loves you, man. I saw it the day she left. Give her time. It's only been a few weeks. It's a good sign she's talking to you at all. I imagine she's more hurt than mad."

I caused that by being a chickenshit and not coming straight out, admitting who my mom was. He's right. I'm in a far better position today with her than I was the day she kicked us out of her hospital room after finding out both Mom and I lied to her.

"Patience is not my thing," I grumble, staring at my ankle, willing it to heal faster. I'm doing everything the doctor ordered. I'm eating well, taking supplements to promote bone growth and healing. I'm taking it easy even though everything inside me is telling me to get my ass to Daisy.

"You waited a year before asking her out. I'd say patience is your super power."

I never thought of it that way. But it's hard to patient when you know what you're missing.

We arrive to Galant charging out to help, though I've got exiting the car down pat. Since the fire, Mom insists on reinstituting the weekly family dinners that had become less and less frequent over the years. Having them again is a good thing.

I can't wait to bring Daisy home to one as soon as she'll let me.

Am I being impatient if I'm counting the seconds until that happens?

CHAPTER 9

THE ONLY GOOD THING ABOUT MY TIME away from Daisy is my focus on getting better, healing in the fastest, healthiest way possible. In all other aspects, it's complete misery. I'd just gotten her, and I turn and lose the woman of my dreams because I kept the truth from her, *and* I sacrificed my life for hers. The latter couldn't be helped, and I'd do it again in a heartbeat. But the former, totally my fault.

I was a dumbass. Plain and simple.

Now another month has passed of daily texts of nothing special since the day I admitted I still love her. I felt her rejection when she didn't say it back, not that I expected her to. Through her anger, I know she still cares, otherwise she would've kicked me to the curb when she left and never looked back. But it's the fact she's still reaching out to connect, not to punish, even if she's mad.

She's still hanging on—in there with me—through thick and thin, I hope. Not just resentment.

"Here you go, Mr. Ashford. Let's see how it feels." The doc returns with a walking boot, having just removed my cast. After fitting it and little adjustment, he looks at his handiwork. "Looks good. Don't push it. You can just as easily reinjure your leg doing too much too soon or forgetting to wear this."

Forget? What idiot forgets to put a walking boot on a near-broken ankle that was just in a cast? Purposely think you can hop a few feet without it and then get hurt? Possibly. "That's not me, Doc. I understand the importance of taking it slow and giving my body the time it needs to heal. I'll wear it religiously until you tell me to stop."

He smiles and pats my shoulder. "I wish all my patients were so level-headed."

Ha! Galant would bust a gut hearing the doc call me that. I'm not considered all that level-headed in his eyes. "I've got a girl to win back, so healing is my priority."

"I have a feeling you're the type of man who gets what he wants, once he puts his mind to it."

"Pretty much." Especially when it comes to my Wildflower. "I'll do anything, Doc. Even if it means taking the time to heal."

"Good man." He checks the chart. "I'll see you back in a month. See how you're progressing. Keep doing your leg exercises at home. I'd plan on starting physical therapy for your ankle after I see you next and then probably release you to work a month after that."

Two months. I can do it.

I *will* do it.

I have no choice if I want to be braw and ready for my girl.

"You must be anxious to get back to work," he adds as he opens the exam room door.

Hmm, I haven't really been focused on that. Kinda surprising, or maybe more telling that I haven't been. "I'm just focused on healing." *And getting my girl back.*

"You're nearly there. Be patient."

His words speak to me more about Daisy than my job or being healthy.

"I'm not messing it up," I promise as I check out and schedule the follow-up. I text Turner *I'm ready* and head downstairs to wait for him to pick me up. Now that I have a boot, I should be able to start driving. Except I need to buy a new truck. Mine was destroyed in the fire when the building collapsed. Daisy's was farther back and didn't have a scratch on it, according to my brothers.

"What the doc say?" He's on me as soon as I get in his car.

"Another month before physical therapy. All good news."

"That's great. Where to?"

"I need to buy a car." I received my insurance check a few weeks ago but didn't feel like car shopping with crutches and a cast. Now that I'm more maneuverable, it seems like the perfect way to celebrate.

"Lunch, then car shopping?" He pulls onto the main thoroughfare.

"Sounds good." I shoot off a text to my Flower and settle in. "We should take lunch to Theo."

"Yeah, that's a great idea." He smiles.

It is. I haven't seen Theo much since I've been less mobile, except at family dinners. Plus, I'm sure she'll have some thoughts on cars—trucks—I should consider. If I gave her time, she'd build me one from the ground up. While motorcycles are more her thing, I can't ride one right now with my boot. Or maybe I could. But honestly, the idea of riding without Daisy on the back just doesn't appeal to me.

"Head to Duke's. I'll let her know we're coming." I text Theo to be sure she hasn't eaten, though I'm nearly a hundred percent sure she hasn't. She still needs a man or someone to take her mind off work, someone who sees her often to help put meat on her bones, remind her of what's important, that there's more to life than work.

"Sounds like a plan."

Daisy reminded me of what's important, what I'm working for, what I want out of life, and the closer I get to returning to work, the more I realize it's not fighting fires.

It's not fear talking. I'm not afraid to go back to work.

I'm afraid of going back to living a passionless life. I don't feel the work like I used to. I haven't since Daisy and I got serious. The moment I set her on that fake balcony to save her life, I was deeply grateful for my knowledge and skills, but knew in my bones it was time for a change. To find a job that is less dangerous and feeds my soul.

I pray I get to find out what that change is with my girl by my side.

"You alright?" Sage comes inside after ushering his group out the door to don their wet suits for their surfing lesson. His eyes land on my shoulder. One of the guys in his class smacked me pretty good with the surfboard he was supposed to leave outside. I wasn't watching, and the guy had no idea he should just back out instead of trying to turn around in such a confined space.

I should be grateful it was my shoulder and not my head or face. "Yeah, I'm fine. I think you're gonna need the patience of a saint."

He chuckles. "Naw, I got this. Groms gotta start somewhere." His eyes fall behind me. "Hey, Dink, don't let her lift anything."

"On it." Dink comes from out back where they primarily work on the boards for rental, sale, or to be repaired. There's also an extension that has an office and living quarters. My dad used to live there on and off through the years, but business has been better, or he's stopped spending everything he banked and hasn't needed to live here, so Dink and Casey live here now. Right on the beach. It's a sweet gig.

"I'll take you to lunch when I get back." Sage pauses at the door. "You good?"

"The Shack?"

He chuckles. "Again? You know we have a lot of great restaurants. You should try 'em."

"I will—"

"But you want The Shack."

"Please. I don't usually beg, but I've been craving their crab boil since we were there last week."

"Fine. I pick next time."

"Deal."

He slips out the door with a shake of his head. For a moment, I see the little boy I remember instead of the man who grew up while I was gone. His pale green eyes are the same as mine, but the depths of them hold experiences I've missed, heartache or disappointments I wasn't here to comfort. He could have called. *I* should have called. Putting distance between Dad's gravity and myself shouldn't have meant I left Sage behind too.

Dink clears his throat, staring at a surf magazine like it might change his life.

I laugh at his silent request. "You can come. But Casey has to stay to watch the shop."

"Yes!"

I motion to the back. "I'm gonna take a break."

"There's an ice pack in the freezer. Lie on the couch till lunch. I'll get you if we get busy. Casey will be back soon."

I take him up on the offer. After I get settled, I check my phone as I felt it vibrate a bit ago.

Reid: *I got my cast off today. I'm in a walking boot.*

I can feel his happiness in every word. He was tired of the crutches. I can only imagine how good it feels to get some of his mobility back.

Me: *Yay! So exciting. How are you celebrating?*

Reid: *Lunch with Turner and Theo. How are you?*

I don't dare mention my shoulder. I made that mistake a few weeks ago when I slipped in the shower trying to reach for the towel I left on the bathroom counter. He called when I stupidly replied to his text that I hurt myself and couldn't talk. He called. It took me twenty minutes to talk him out of driving here to see for himself that I was alright. Not that he knows where *here* is. And not that he was even able to drive.

Me: *Good. Working. Going to The Shack for lunch after Sage finishes his lesson.*

Reid: *You really like that place, huh? Maybe you'll take me when I visit.*

Me: *If I have to, I'll sacrifice for you.*

Nope, I can't say that. It's too teasing, taunting. *Erase.*
Me: *Maybe.*

Reid: *Don't pretend you wouldn't eat there every day if you could.*

I would. Some people are foodies, like to try new places, new foods all the time, take pictures and post them on social media. I'm not like that. I'm a simple girl. I find something I like, I stick to it. I'm not adventuresome. Food is love, and I don't want to waste love—or food—when I already know what I like.

Me: *Truth.*

Reid: *We're here. I have to go. TTYL?*

Me: *Yep. Enjoy your family.*

I hide my disappointment behind closed eyes and set my

phone on my chest. I miss him more and more each day. I thought it would be the opposite: absence would make my heart forget, make it easier, but nothing feels easier. In fact, most things feel harder since I've moved here. Just getting out of bed most days is an exercise in self-motivation. Eating, showering, being social at the shop—all feel like a chore. So much effort I never had to give before. It all came so naturally, easily.

Now, nothing is easy. Did I take it all for granted? Or have I changed, and it really is harder?

CHAPTER 10

"I REALLY CAN'T." I SEND SAGE A PLEADING look when the guy who keeps asking me out each time he comes in the shop—which is way more than he really needs to, I'm sure—won't take no for an answer to end the conversation. Again.

"Sorry, Perry, my sister has a boyfriend." Sage narrows his gaze, not happy to bail me out when he thinks I should be saying *yes*. Maybe not to this guy but to *someone*.

"You should have said so." The guy frowns, grabbing his bag of surf wax he bought, and scurries out.

"I didn't want to be rude," I holler after him, drawing the attention of the other customers milling around. I don't really have a boyfriend, do I? It seemed wrong to pretend to belong to Reid when I'm keeping him at arm's length just so this guy would leave me alone.

"You should say yes. He's a nice guy," Sage suggests.

"He's a dweeb. You can do better, Daisy." Chase kisses my cheek, wiggling his eyebrows as if he's offering himself as an option.

I had better.

Sage's glare sweeps to him. "Don't touch my sister."

"Whoa, brother bear, just a little fun." Chase slips out back.

"You don't have fun with my sister." Sage's disapproving tone follows Chase.

"He's harmless." And flirtatious.

"You should go out with *someone*." He points behind me. "Not with Chase or Dink."

"I'm not going out with anyone."

"Why? Because of *him*? It's been months. If he cared so much, he'd be here."

"He doesn't know where I am." We've had this discussion before. Of course it's because of Reid. I may not have forgiven him or his mom, but I'm not about to move on and start dating. I'm not even fully healed yet. Granted I'm the one who left, but it would feel like I'm betraying him if I started dating other guys, especially when we feel... unfinished.

"I doubt he's pining, waiting around on you," Sage grates. This feels personal, more than a brother worrying about his sister pining for a guy who doesn't deserve it. His words, not mine.

"Wow. Who pissed in your Cheerios this morning?" Grumpy is not his go-to attitude. Something is up.

"No one." He swipes the keys for the company truck. "I need to make a supply run. Catch ya later." He disappears out the front door before I can question him further. His intent, I'm sure. Whatever's bothering him, he doesn't want to talk about it.

When the last customer leaves, I take a break, grab a water, and head out back to the porch swing off the living quarters. It's peaceful, surrounded by plants and not easily seen by those just passing by.

The idea that Reid might be dating someone else lingers in my thoughts.

I. Left. Him.

He has every right to move on, even if I'm praying he hasn't. It's not fair. I know.

But I've spent so much time trying to convince myself what happened between the two of us wasn't wholly real because he kept the secret that Mary was his mother. I don't trust my feelings nor his.

I finger my phone, tempted. Letting out a rush of air, I set my phone on the seat beside me and take a drink.

Do I ask him? Do I have a right? It's been two and a half months. He doesn't even text me as often as he used to.

He's totally moved on.

Me: *Hey.*

Stellar start.

Reid: *Hey yourself. What's up?*

He sounds like he's in a good mood.

Me: *Question.*

Reid: *Shoot.*

My confidence wavers as I consider if I really want to know the answer to the question I'm about to ask.

Me: *Are you dating?*

Reid: *What?*

Me: *Women. Are you seeing other women?*

Dang, my eyes prick with looming tears. I hold my phone to my chest as I swing and stare into the distance. *Please say no.*

I nearly scream when my phone rings. "H-hello."

"What the fuck, Flower?"

He's angry?

"Am I not allowed to ask?" Maybe I lost the right to know anything about his life. Did I take the push-pull too far, unintentionally?

I'm so confused. The longer I'm away, the more lost I feel. The stronger my body gets, the weaker I am—I want to run back. I don't know what I'm doing here anymore. It seemed so clear, but now, I'm racked with uncertainty.

"No!" he barks, then sighs. "Yes. Yes, you can ask. But you shouldn't have to."

"I should just know?"

"Yes. Dammit."

My heart pounds in my chest. Anxiety tightens my throat, locking up my voice. *I should know?*

"Daisy, tell me you know I don't want anyone else but you."

His gruff, commanding voice sends goosebumps along my skin, but it's his words that ping in my chest.

"I—"

"Do you want to date other guys? Is that what this is about?"

When I don't answer, because I can't, he sighs and waits a few more seconds. "What do I always say?"

"Take what I need," I whisper.

"That's right. And what do you need, baby?" His anger is gone, but the need is ever present in his tone.

I can practically feel him pressing me against the wall with his larger-than-life body, heating me up, seeking truth in the depth of my eyes, and breathing hope and love into my melancholy existence. "You."

"Then we're on the same page. 'Cause all I need is you, Flower."

Then why is he there and I'm here? I swipe at my silly tears I shouldn't be crying. I did this to us. He didn't want me to leave, and now we're broken just as we've healed.

"What happened?" He draws me back to him.

"Nothing. Just a bad day."

"You feeling alright?"

"Yeah."

"Talk to me, baby. Tell me what's going on in that beautiful head of yours."

"I can't." I'm a pitiful wreck.

He sighs in exasperation. "I hate this distance. Tell me where you are. I'm coming to see you."

"No!" I jump to my feet, panicked at the idea of him seeing me in such a state. "I'm not ready." I'm an emotional wreck half the time. I don't know what I'm going to do for a living. I'm just now able to climb the stairs to my apartment without having to take a breather. I'm not ready to have to choose him or not—forgive him or not.

"Wildflower, you're driving me crazy here. You say you want me. You won't let me talk to you about what happened. You won't let me apologize. You won't let me come to you. I just want to hold you even if I can't say a word. I want us to be together again."

"One more month." I can get my head on straight in one more month.

"I've started physical therapy. I'll get released to go back to work in three weeks. I could spend all that time with you, working things out, making sure you know the last thing I want is to date anyone else."

He's going back to work. Fighting fires. The idea has me breaking into a cold sweat.

"Daisy?"

"Yeah, I—" I try to calm my nerves with deep breaths and sit down. "You're going back."

"I'm a firefighter. You know that. I might be able to do something else eventually, but for now, my guys are depending on me to come back. They rely—"

"No. No. I know. I just… hadn't thought it through." Of course he'd go back. He loves it. His whole family are firefighters. It's in his blood.

"I wish you'd let me come see you. We could work it all out. I know it."

79

"Three weeks. You can come in three weeks before you go back to work."

"That won't leave us much time." He's disappointed.

Can I can handle him putting his life on the line day in and day out? The fire in my apartment and store put it all into perspective. How much he's willing to sacrifice. He was willing to die to save me. Will he do it again to save a stranger? His brothers?

A chill runs up my spine. I already know the answer.

Of course he would. That's who he is.

And who am I? Am I even the girl he fell for? I don't feel the same. I feel like a zombie most of the time—except with him.

"It's the best I can do." I need off the phone before I have a complete breakdown.

"Then I'll make it work. I'm not screwing this up, Flower. I'll be there where and when you say. Just no dating other guys, okay?"

"I never intended on going out with anyone else."

"Good. Me neither. I lo—"

"Don't," I cut him off, feeling like a beotch. I can't hear him say it and stay strong in this moment.

Strong. Who am I kidding? I'm so far from strong, it's pitiful.

"Talk soon, baby." Thankfully he drops it.

"Bye, Reid." I hang up and go back inside. I'm getting paid to work, not mope over my maybe-used-to-be boyfriend.

Three weeks.

Can I make it?

CHAPTER 11

THE TIME AWAY FROM DAISY IS DRIVING ME to push harder in therapy and working with my mom. I started tending her garden—more like overseeing it—so she can focus on the Flower Mart. Mom runs herself ragged most days. I know she was hopeful she could convince Daisy to come on board to share the workload before the fire at Daisy's shop, before Daisy and I even started dating. Now that Daisy's lost her shop, Mom is even more determined it's meant to be, if only Daisy would forgive us and come home.

Come home, Flower. I miss you.

My heart aches continuously as if it's threatening to stop

beating unless I make it right, make amends, bring my girl home to our home, our bed, our life we were just starting together.

Martin, my mom's full-time employee, has the patience of a saint. I come and go. Some days are good. Others, not so much. He has other employees, so really, I'm just a big inconvenience most days. But getting my hands dirty, feeling the earth under my nails, planting the seeds that grow into the beautiful blooms my mom and girl love, it settles something deep inside.

I have vague memories of helping my mom as a little kid before my brothers pulled me away to play *manlier* types of games or sports. When football took root, it was all I could think about. I'd still help Mom when she asked, but I no longer tagged along because it was what I wanted to do. It became an obligation to make her happy.

As the sun hits the horizon, I look up, stretching my neck and back. I take a few deep breaths before heading to the outdoor basin to wash my hands and face. If Martin's wife Suzy wasn't around, I'd strip and let the cool water from the hose wash away the grime of the day. I settle for washing my upper body and soaking my head, then stare out across the blooming fields of flowers and let the thoughts I've been keeping at bay all day flood me.

Is Daisy outside today enjoying the sun?

Has anyone asked her out?

Is that why she asked me if I've moved on?

Is she tempted to say *yes*?

Will she forgive me?

Do I deserve it?

Is she watching the same sunset at this very moment?

Drying off my hands I unlock my phone to text her but already see a text waiting for me.

Wildflower: *Hypothetical Question…*

Wildflower: *How would it make you feel if you never saw me again?*

My heart skips. *Never saw her again? What is she sayin'?*

Me: *Are you trying to tell me something?*

Me: *If this is supposed to be funny. It's not.*

The gravel crunches below my boots as I eat up the distance to my truck. Any calm I felt a moment ago thinking we could be sharing the same sunset, seeps away.

How would I feel?

Miserable.

Like I do now.

Have I lost her?

My phone chimes, but I can't look. Not yet. I need a cold drink and privacy for this conversation. She's pulling away, further than she already has.

Hypothetical my ass.

If she thinks throwing me questions like that will drive me off, making herself look high maintenance and needy, she's mistaken. I crave her neediness, her wanting to hear how much I want her, need her, love her. Yet, she won't even let me say any of those things. She's closed herself off from me. Forcing me to live with this physical and emotional distance while still reaching out.

Hope is starting to hurt, but I refuse to quit.

She said she needed three weeks. I think time is up.

If this is a call for help, an SOS, then pack my bags, I'm coming, baby.

"Reid?" Mom stops me before I open my door. "You heading out?" She eases off the back porch of my parents' house, wiping her hands on her apron as she nears. "I thought you might stay for dinner. Theo is coming over."

"Do you know where she is?"

"Who… Daisy?" She frowns as I nod. "No, she's upset with me too. Remember?"

"Yeah, I just thought she might have reached out to you just so you'd know she was safe."

Her eyes crinkle in the corners as her brow lowers. "Sadly, no."

"I've got to find her."

"You have any idea where she is?"

"She's not too far, maybe a few hours up the coast. Her father has a surf shop."

Mom smiles. "You know who her dad is, right?"

"No." Why should I? She barely talked about her family, other than her brother Sage. I was surprised she was staying with her dad, considering they didn't have that close of a relationship.

"He's Robbie Webb."

My eyes bug out. "The surf god?"

"One and the same."

"How do you know this?" And I don't? Why wouldn't Daisy tell me who her dad is?

"Stay for dinner, and I'll tell you." She pats my arm. "It's too late to head out now. You need daylight when hunting for flowers."

I check my phone for the hundredth time. He never replied to my last text. It's been hours. The text doesn't even show as read. I guess I really did piss him off. Which wasn't my intention.

Or was it? Did I only send it to get a rise out of him?

I pace my small apartment, contemplating why I really sent it, considering the state of our relationship.

I left him.

I pushed him away.

Now I'm asking how he'd feel if he *never* saw me again.

Yeah, that was a bad idea. I saw it on someone's social and thought it was a good conversation starter, but given the lack of real talking we've been doing—my fault—it wasn't fair to ask casually. But I needed to know.

It's like begging for compliments but without going first. I was begging him to tell me how he feels, even though he's been trying to tell me for months.

I'm an idiot.

But he lied to me… though it doesn't justify me playing text games, trying to get a rise out of him.

I shoot off another text.

Me: *Forget my question. It was thoughtless of me to ask. I'm sorry.*

When thirty minutes pass and he still hasn't answered, I kinda panic.

Me: *Can we just forget it?*

Nothing. No response. He hasn't even read any of my follow-up texts. He's really mad, and it's all my fault.

If it wasn't so late, and if I didn't have to open the shop in the morning, I'd consider driving to apologize in person.

What if something happened?

What if he was so mad, he was distracted by my text and got into a car wreck?

What if he's decided I'm not worth the effort, drama, or pain in the tush?

I fall into bed, knowing it's going to be a long, sleepless night. How can I fix this?

I keep checking my phone.

It keeps being silent, mocking me and my stupidity.

CHAPTER 12

GETTING TO WORK BEFORE THE SUN IS EVEN up was my norm for years with the flower shop, but I've gotten lazy. Today, I feel like the walking dead as I drive the short distance to Dad's shop before the sun even hits the horizon. I'll definitely need a few cups of coffee before I feel remotely human—or awake.

Would Reid be disappointed to know I drink coffee now instead of our healthy smoothies? I'm not sure I care. It's the only thing that keeps me out of bed. It used to be looking forward to the day and then it was looking forward to seeing him on Tuesdays and nearly every day after when we finally admitted how we felt and got together. I'm still in awe that he liked me all that time I was crushing on him.

That version of myself feels so far off. A millennium ago, at least. I miss her hopeful, buoyant energy.

My phone was still silent when my alarm went off, though I had only fallen asleep a few hours earlier. I checked it way too often in the middle of the night. At least I resisted texting him again. Apologizing *again*.

His silence feeds my fears. He's given up. I pushed one too many times. I was a silly girl needing reassurance he was all too willing to give, but instead of letting him just say what he's been wanting to all these months, I played a game of *tell me how much it'll hurt to lose me.*

Childish, immature games.

If he stays silent all day, I'm calling him tonight. And if he won't talk to me, then I'll drive to him. And if he *still* won't talk to me, I'm not afraid to get down and dirty—I'll go to Mary. She may be his mom, but she was my friend before he was my boyfriend. She'll have some pull to get him to see me face-to-face.

Whatever it takes.

Except no more childish games.

It's time to grow up, face my fears, decide what my next steps are beyond getting him to talk to me. Do I want to reopen my shop? Should I see if Mary will take me on, even if only part-time?

As important as a job is, it all seems inconsequential when I think about never seeing Reid again. I asked him how he'd feel about that. But I hadn't truly considered it. I'd feel dead inside. Hopeless wrapped in anguish over losing what I was so close to having forever. If I'd just given him the time of day to say his piece, we could be together now.

Casey greets me when I unlock the front door. Startled, I stumble back. "Casey! What... I thought you were off this morning." I breathe a little deeper as I reenter, closing and locking the door till we're ready to open.

"Yeah, sorry about that. I should have called you. It was a last-minute change. You can go back to bed if you want." He points to the back. "You can even take my bed." He smirks. "I don't mind."

"Uh, no." The last thing I want to do is climb in a bed that smells like any man other than Reid. I shudder at the thought. "I'm already up. I'd rather work and get off early." Now that I'm here. Had he called me on the way over, I absolutely would have turned around. "Next time, call me, no matter the time."

"Sure. Sorry." I hand him a five. "You're getting the coffee this morning."

He pockets the money and continues to open the register. But his eyes meet mine when he feels my heavy stare. "Oh, you mean now?"

"Yes. I need coffee if I'm going to survive this morning."

"You mean if *I'm* going to survive this morning?" He chuckles as he heads for the door.

"*You* surviving is still debatable."

He laughs. "Damn, I'm going to miss you when you leave."

I stop and blink at him. *Am I leaving?*

Casey stills. "I mean *if* you leave."

"Do you know something I don't?" Is Dad tired of me already? He's barely here. That can't be it. Am I the reason he stays away?

Casey shakes his head, smiling. "Naw, you're not like your dad, Sage, or the rest of us. Surfing isn't your thing. You had a life before you got hurt. You'll want to go back to it soon enough."

With that bomb dropped, he leaves. The door quietly closes behind him. The only sound comes from the air conditioner, the breaking morning waves, and the *thump, thump, thump,* of my heart.

Turning to the back counter, I work on the folding billboard for outside, using my creative juices to give this week's specials a little more flair.

Sage gives a quick, "Good morning," as he enters the front to disappear to the back, prepping for his morning's lessons. He's also training a new employee, Tabitha, who should be here any minute. Dad says she's a promising surfer, looking to go pro, but in the meantime, she needs to earn money for her entrance fees.

Dad has always been a sucker for any and all surfers. Good or bad, you're welcome in the realm of Robbie Webb. And if you need a job and are willing to work, he'll give you one even if he doesn't need help. When I was a kid, Mom would complain about Dad taking in strays and paying them a weekly wage he couldn't afford.

Now, he can afford it. After the career he's had, surfboards with his name on them, and branded gear sold all over the world, not just in his shop, he can afford to close shop and live the rest of his life off the royalties alone. But surfing is in his blood. He has no intention of sitting back and missing out on all the fun.

If it wasn't for Sage and his business and marketing degree, Dad wouldn't be where he is today. The last few years the business has really taken off. He's talking about opening additional shops in California and Hawaii, and eventually Australia. Sage will have his hands full trying to reel Dad in, if he doesn't get swept up in the excitement too. It's a good thing Sage loves it as much as Dad. As much as I know Dad is his own person and will be fine no matter what, I'm happy he's finally found financial success—for him and for Sage.

The ding of the door chime means my coffee has arrived. Keeping my eyes on my handiwork, I decide to add a border. "It's about time. A girl could fall asleep waiting for you to bring her her morning caffeine."

When he doesn't reply, the silence is deafening as the back of my neck prickles with recognition. I'm brought back to those lovely Tuesday mornings when *he'd* step into my flower shop, carrying the weight of the world on his shoulders with ease as if his job wasn't life or death on any given day. One gruff response, focused gaze, would right my world I didn't know was off-kilter.

My Sequoia. But it can't be—

"Um, Daisy, there's a hulk of a guy blatantly staring at the back of your head like he wants to consume you in one bite." Sage leans against the door frame, arms crossed, not a bit concerned about the size of the man stealing all the air in the room. "Do you have a lot of stalkers back home?"

"He's not…" I swallow and close my eyes as I take a breath and stand straight. "I know who it is," I whisper as his heavy steps advance, sending a shiver along my spine.

"Flower." The grate in his voice in person couldn't be more thrilling.

God, I've missed him—missed his *I've been eating bark for breakfast* timbre.

Slowly, I turn. One hand grips the counter for support I'm sure to need.

The second our eyes connect, I lose all composure as his heated gaze eats me up from the other side of the counter. Chin trembling, I come face-to-face with the man who left me on that flimsy ledge to live while locking himself inside my burning apartment.

He left me.

He saved me.

He sacrificed for me.

I've held on to my anger about him and Mary lying about their relationship for too long. At this moment, in his presence, I'm not even sure that's what I was mad about. Or if I'm mad at all. I'm afraid of losing him to his job, to his courage, to his selflessness. I'm afraid of loving him and losing him in a snap of a finger, in a flash of a flame.

The sob I've been holding back erupts. I clamp my hand over my mouth to temper my imminent meltdown.

He reaches me faster than a man in his condition should be able to. I barely get a glimpse of his walking boot before I'm swept in his arms. His gruff, "Daisy," has the dam breaking. He only holds me tighter, asking, "Where, baby?"

"Out back." Sage must guide him as Reid moves like he knows where he's going.

WILDFIRE

When I feel the light ocean breeze sweeping across my back, I dare a second look at my Sequoia. Dark hair, the perfect tan, clenched jaw, delectable lips, strong nose, and soulful caramel eyes. He's perfect in his rugged, *not afraid to take a punch in the face* demeanor. He's all man, and I'm wild for him.

He sits me on the porch railing, my back to the ocean, I'm barely registering if the sun is rising, or if it's him bringing all the light back into my life.

CHAPTER 13

I SWIPE AT HER TEARS THAT BREAK MY HEART with each falling drop. "Daisy," I press soft kisses across her wet cheeks, mumbling, "please don't cry."

"I thought you were done with me," she blubbers, crying harder the more she tries to hold tough.

I pull her tight, wrapping her in my arms. "No. Never done." Never. Never. Never. Done.

"But you—"

"Shh, don't talk. Just know that I'm here because what I have to say can't be said through text or over the phone." I cup her face. "I'm done waiting, Wildflower. I've come to bring you home where you belong."

"You are?" New tears spring free.

"I got you." I pick her up, encouraging her to wrap around me. "I'm taking you to your place, but you're going to have to give me directions."

The guy who must be her brother is there the moment I step inside with my girl wrapped around me like a spider monkey. I still, long enough to gauge his reaction. "I'm taking her home."

"I'm guessing you're Reid?"

"Her boyfriend, yeah. You Sage?"

"Yep. Her brother." His smile is crooked and mischievous as he states his place in her life as I did. "Here." He hands me a purse. "I'm sure she'll want it. I kept her key fob. We'll drop her car by later."

"Thanks." I want to thank him for taking care of my girl. But knowing her, she took care of herself and wouldn't appreciate me giving the credit to someone else. Particularly another man, who, as far as I know, never visited her for as long as she lived in my town.

We're exiting the door I entered mere minutes ago afraid my girl wouldn't greet me warmly. I couldn't be happier with her response. I'd rather she wasn't crying, but I'll take it over being angry and distant.

She missed me. I can work with that.

We need to talk, but that may test me more than I anticipated, given I'm hard as a rock with her in my arms. All I want to do is get her home, in bed, naked, and under me so I can reintroduce her to the depth of my love.

"If we're going to talk, I'll need coffee," she manages as I set her in the passenger seat of my truck. Her pale green eyes shimmer with unshed tears as she looks up with vulnerability and want.

"I'll get you anything you need."

"You and coffee." She stretches, pressing her tear-soaked lips to mine. She's hesitant and ends the kiss too quickly before I've barely registered the sweetness of her. "But coffee first."

"Coffee coming up." I tip her chin, not questioning why she's drinking coffee now when she didn't before. "But first, I need a proper taste."

Her breath hitches as I kiss the gasp from her lips, stealing her tongue, sucking softly before releasing her with another quick press of our mouths.

It's not enough, but it'll have to do.

Pulling into her driveway, I eye the stairs leading up to her apartment above the garage. "Is your father home?" I didn't see him at the surf shop, so he could be here.

She twists her lips, looking over her shoulder at the quiet house. "I have no idea. I don't see him but a couple of times a week, usually at breakfast."

I undo her seatbelt and then mine. "He doesn't come to his shop?"

"Um, not usually." She fidgets a second and glances out the windshield. "Will the steps be a problem with your boot?"

"No." I open my door, get out, and turn to find her eyes still on me. "Though I don't think I should attempt to carry you like I'd planned."

A soft smile breaks the melancholy riddling her beautiful features. "You have a thing for carrying me, don't you?"

Blood rages to my cock. "I have a thing for having you in my arms, in whatever form that takes, Flower." I pin her with my stare. "Stay put."

Closing my door, I open the back and sling my bag over my shoulder. I came to get her, but I figure I can give her a few days—a week—to come to terms with it and come willingly. Not that I won't consider dragging her home with a heavy persuasion of the tongue. And by *dragging*, I mean making her come on my tongue until she begs me to take her wherever I wish and where she truly *wants* to be. In our bed—at *our* home.

"You sure?" She glances from my boot to the top of the stairs and back.

"I'm sure." I release her hand to pat her butt. "You first." I may not be able to safely carry her cradled in my arms, but when she hesitates, I add, "I could always throw you over my shoulder. Fireman style."

"Uh, no. I'm good." She digs in her purse, I assume for her keys, as she ascends the staircase, providing me an excellent view. She's thinner than when I saw her last. I'm sad to think I had anything to do with keeping her from enjoying life and food as she used to, but her ass and every inch of her is deliciously tempting.

At the top of the stairs, I fit to her back and still her hand before she turns the knob. "I need you to know before we step

97

inside that there's nothing you can say or do to make me not want a future with you. I know we have lots to discuss, but I don't want you fearing the outcome. No matter how messy the middle gets, I'm still here for the finish."

"OhmyholyGrandmaJean," she whispers as she leans into me, her head falling to my shoulder. "You have no idea how much I needed to hear that."

Yeah, I do. I wish she could say the same. But I'm not the one who was hurt by keeping secrets. She needs to hear my words before she can make such a promise.

I kiss her neck and twist the doorknob, her hand still grasping it like a lifeline. "I got you, Wildflower."

CHAPTER 14

WHEN WE STEP INTO MY APARTMENT, I'M flooded with memories of the first time he was in my place above my flower shop. My Sequoia takes up a lot of space in size and presence. I'm surprised his head doesn't graze the ceiling as he continues to my bedroom like he's been here before—like he belongs among my things.

He does. The thought hits like a ton of bricks, reminding me what a silly girl I've been. Over three months I've missed being with him, healing *with* him, loving and being loved *by* him.

The ball of nerves that tightened in my gut the moment I *felt* him enter the surf shop loosens. My shoulders drop, and I take a full breath for the first time since... Well, it feels like forever.

Sans bag, he leans against the doorjamb, arms crossed, emphasizing his impressive muscles as he scans me from my feet to my head, coming back to lock eyes. "You need me to show you."

I stutter a step toward him. "What?"

Languidly, he unfolds his arms and covers the distance between us, tipping my chin to keep my attention as if I could look anywhere else even if I wanted to. "You need a reminder." He grazes my jaw with his mouth, laving kissing to my ear and back, sealing his lips to mine. A lazy lick, a gruff command, "Open," and I'm putty in his hands.

His tender kiss turns to starving the second our tongues meet. Growling, I'm enfolded in his massive arms, squeezing and kneading my backside with his powerful, cajoling hands.

"Reid," is all I can manage between kisses and gasps as his mouth traverses my neck to my shoulder and back, eating up my moans as I plead, "more."

"Take what you need," he growls into my neck as he picks me up by my thighs, encouraging me to wrap my legs around him.

His hardness presses to my soft center, and I nearly die a thousand deaths grinding against him, trying to get him closer, inside me, despite our clothing. My heart hurts, the ache too much to bear, the distance, the cruelty of my anger and fear.

What did it serve?

What purpose?

"Please," I beg. Tears fall as my hurt mixes with need to never let him go.

"Flower." He gently lowers me to the bed, coming down with me, his hands softening the fall before bracketing my face. "Please," he kisses my cheeks, "please don't cry. I'm here. We're here. We're together. We can work through it all, just let me love you. Let me *show* you."

Yes. Yes. A million times, "Yes."

Action speaking louder than words, my man strips bare as he caresses me with his eyes and seduces me with his dirty talk, rendering me a squirming mess by the time he has to stop to deal with his boot. Sitting on the edge of the bed, bent forward, he pins me with his heated gaze over his shoulder. "Naked. Now, Daisy."

I make quick work of my clothing, too turned on to be self-conscious or consider that maybe my shower last night wasn't recent enough.

"Jesus." He captures my hand pulling me to him, but instead of sequestering me in his lap as anticipated, he sets me on the edge of the bed facing away from him. "Daisy," his voice cracks as his fingers trail over my left shoulder and down, circling my scar where the rod entered my back, fracturing ribs and puncturing a lung.

"I'm okay," I reassure, catching his watery gaze over my shoulder. My ribs still ache at times, and my lung capacity seems less, but it could be psychosomatic. I'm afraid to breathe too deeply in fear of reopening the wound.

"It barely missed your heart." The depth of his remorse only amplifies my desire to make things right.

I've felt so alone, remote, cut off from everything I love and hold dear. My livelihood, my friends—him. Being home hasn't been the same. My sadness doused every potential joy until I lost my smile and my zest for life.

He didn't do that.

I did it. I let what happened turn everything sour.

I never imagined I was only one tragedy away from life-altering depression.

"Did it miss my heart?" I face him, palming his stubble-rough jaw. "Physically, *yes*. But in every other way imaginable, I've been without my heart ever since."

"You died." He presses his forehead to mine. "I jumped out the window not knowing what I'd find when I heard the balcony break and you screaming as you fell."

I squeeze my eyes tightly shut, trying to block it out. The fear, the belief I'd never see him again comes flooding in. "You left me by sacrificing yourself."

"I had no choice." His voice is rough with emotion. "It was the only way I could save you." His grip on me tightens. "You weren't breathing. So I breathed for you until the ambulance arrived."

"You saved me. I know you did, but you could have died, and where would I be without you?"

He pulls me into his lap. "I keep running it through my mind: *What could I have done differently?* But each time, I come to the same conclusion. I had to set you out there on the fake balcony, praying it would hold you."

Praying it would hold you. It didn't.

I fell. But we're both still here.

He jumped, broke his ankle and still managed to get to me. Bring me back to life, keeping me alive until help came. He survived for the both of us.

"Promise you won't do that again."

Rearing back, his scowl meets my determined gaze. "What?

Save you? I can't promise you that, Daisy. I'll give my last breath to keep you living."

He gave so much, and I've hardly been living. "I'm barely alive without you," I whisper across his lips.

He presses his mouth to mine, moving slowly, sucking my top lip, then my bottom. "Let me remind you what living feels like."

CHAPTER 15

SQUEEZE AND KNEAD HER ASS, SPREADING her cheeks, and she moans into our kiss. Reluctantly, I break off, panting, "Daisy?"

Her slow blink is adorable as she tries to focus. "Yeah?"

"Let me love you." I slide my hand lower, touching her intimately as if her naked on my lap with my cock between us isn't intimate enough or a green light to continue, yet I need her words.

"I didn't think it was a question." She rolls her hips, sighing as her head falls back when my fingers graze her opening. Despite her aroused state, she locks on me, leaning in, pressing soft kisses to my jaw, gasping when I slip a finger inside her. "Take what you need."

Those are my words, but I don't mind her giving them back to me. If she thinks for a second I won't take everything she's willing to give, she'd be wrong. But this right here, her riding my hand, her wet folds teasing my cock as she pants her desire across my face, our lips barely touching, is nearly too much and yet not nearly enough. "Ride me, Flower. Put my cock inside you and take what you need."

"Reid, that mouth of yours—"

"Is going to be on you in ten seconds if you don't..."

She lifts, dislodging my finger, and slowly slides down my length. *Jesus Christ.*

"Ohmy—"

I cover her mouth. "Please don't talk about your Grandma Jean while you're taking my cock."

She nods, biting her lip as she sinks lower. "Oh, I... God."

"Fuck." Nothing has ever felt so good or right. I won't last long if it feels this good and she hasn't even moved. "Baby." I grip her ass and the back of her neck, bringing her mouth to mine, urging her, "Ride me good and hard, Wildflower."

"Ye—" Whatever she was going to say dies in our kiss as she slams her mouth to mine and grips the back of my neck and shoulder. She starts to grind and thrust.

Her hungry moans and needful tongue bring me to the brink of insanity as she picks up the pace, riding me fast and hard.

Just like I asked. *Commanded.*

Every forward thrust has her gasping into my mouth, one long, endless kiss I won't let her break except to release her moans and suck in air.

Faster.

Harder.

Jesus. "Fuck, baby." If I ever thought I knew how wild my Wildflower could be, I was thankfully mistaken. This. This is—

"Reid, fu—" she gasps, arching, her head falling back as she slams forward over and over again.

I seize her tit, lifting it to my mouth, and suck, nibbling and teasing her supple nipple. She cries out, chanting my name.

Christ. She's good for the ego, though she's the one doing all the work. "Take it, baby." *Take what you need.*

Her nails dig into my flesh as her pussy squeezes my cock, barely letting go when she pulls back and sucks me deep with each forward thrust.

Not gonna last.

Fuck.

Too damn good.

"Daisy," I warn, which isn't really a warning at all other than letting her know I'm about to blow my load, and if she doesn't want it inside her—

"I want to feel you come." Our eyes lock. She cups my cheek. Tender. So fucking tender. "I want you to let go."

"Baby." This is our first time. I can't—

"I'm not afraid of what you're holding back."

"I don't want to hurt you. We're still healing."

"You won't hurt me."

I glance at her left shoulder. "Yeah, I will." I kiss the front that doesn't reflect the damage on her back or internally. I can't rail her without jarring her shoulder. Besides, I'm not missing anything. She's blowing my mind. But she doubts. "Daisy, I don't need more than you're giving me. I'm not holding back. I'm right here."

She nods and stills. "But you like to be in control."

Running my fingers through the back of her hair, I grip her neck, garnering her eyes. "I gave you control. Your pleasure is my pleasure. Sometimes you'll drive, and others, I will. Make no mistake, I'm one thousand percent here giving you everything I have."

She tries to look away. I tighten my grip, drawing her gaze back to me. There's something else going on. She was ready to come. I felt it. Fuck, I was nearly there myself.

"Are you punishing yourself? Is that what this is?" I don't have any other explanation why she put the brakes on.

"What?! No." She again tries to avert her gaze.

"Daisy, do you think your pleasure is less important than mine? You were about to come. You're still fluttering around my cock. You're primed to blow. I could rub you to an orgasm in seconds."

"I..." One tear slips down her check and then another.

"Talk to me."

"I left you." Her admission brings more tears.

Yeah, she did. It stings that she pushed me away so easily. Yet I was wrong. It wasn't easy for her at all. She's been suffering here all along—alone.

"You had good reasons to be upset. Me leaving you on that ledge felt like I abandoned you, and then you got hurt on top of that. Then hours later you felt betrayed when you found out Mary is my mother."

She nods but stays silent. Words shimmer in the back of her eyes.

"Tell me."

"I don't deserve you. You saved me. You sacrificed for me. You broke your ankle—"

"Fractured," I clarify. Though I do have pins to give it stability due to my size and my job. My body takes a beating.

"You followed your instincts. What you've been trained to do, and all I could think was that you left me to die alone. I didn't consider that *you* were the one who was truly left to die alone. All I could focus on was the idea of not having you here and what that meant."

"It would've been selfish of me to keep you with me when I could ensure your safety. I could save you." I knew that for certain. "I wouldn't have died in there, Daisy. I would have jumped as a last resort if my crew didn't make it in time."

"You did anyway."

"Not in time to keep you from falling. From dying..." I wrap around her, hugging her tight. The fear of losing her comes rushing back. "Don't leave me again. I lost you three times that night. Once when I set you on the balcony, a second time when you fell, and again when you forced me out of your room. I don't blame you for any of it. So please don't blame yourself."

"But—"

"No buts. The fire and all that followed is in the past. I'm sorry I didn't tell you about Mom. We can talk about it more, but I'd rather not with you riding my cock. Which you are, by the way, going to finish and you're going to finish *first*." I flex my hips in emphasis.

She gasps, closing her eyes as her walls flutter around me. *God, that's good.*

"Kiss me?" she asks as if there's a possibility I wouldn't.

CHAPTER 16

H E WAS RIGHT, AND DESPITE BEING UPSET, and our serious discussion, I'm still on the edge. He could blow on my clit, and I think I'd come. Though, honestly, it's probably the idea of him putting his mouth on me that's getting me there.

"Fuck, Daisy. You're so hot. I could watch you ride me all night." His grip on my hips tightens.

All night? My thighs burn, and I can hardly catch my breath. I'm too out of shape for *all night* anything. But, God, do I want to come.

"Take it," he orders, squeezing my ass, urging me on.

Each thrust sends him deep, hitting some magical spot,

and each outswing, his crown rubs my G-spot. It's a double whammy that has me tingling and quivering on the brink of exploding or dying. It's a tossup.

I can't catch my breath.

I don't care if I ever get another one. I just—

"Please," I beg to the god in front of me. "Reid."

"You need help, baby?" His gruff voice shivers up my spine, followed by his hand gripping the back of my neck, squeezing slightly, making me arch so my breasts are in his face. "You feel so good, your juices covering my cock, gripping me so damn tight as you ride me."

"Ugh!" The tingles start.

"That's it, squeeze me with that beautiful pussy. Come all over me, Wildflower."

"Reid!"

"Come. Now," he barks as he swells inside me.

He's going to come.

The realization flings me over the edge, screaming, shuddering, holding on for dear life, I come all over him as he commanded just as he moans his own release, all while praising me, squeezing my breasts, teasing my nipples, and laving me with warm, sultry kisses.

When I finally still but continue to quake with tremors, he gently moves us to the top of the bed, his grip on my ass ensuring he doesn't slip out. As he rolls us to our sides, my bad shoulder up, he tenderly runs his fingers along my cheek and jaw. "You okay?"

"Yeah. You?"

His smile is salacious. "Yeah, Flower. I'm good." He squeezes my ass and flexes his hips. "Not near done loving you."

OhmyholyGrandmaJean. My insides flutter at the thought.

"Mmm, felt that." He rises, rolling me enough to suck a nipple in his mouth, sliding his hand lower, slowly rubbing my clit.

I arch, giving into his ministrations, letting my leg fall open, giving him room to lift his thigh to fall between mine and his cock to surge deeper.

Slowly.

Slowly.

He loves on me.

Gently.

Gently.

He whispers across my skin how good I feel, how amazing sex is with me. *Me.* That alone is enough to have me coming, which I do two more times before he finds his own release and fills me with languid strokes and sensuous kisses, and a grip on my breast that's sure to leave a mark.

"Fuck, Daisy," I groan as I grip her hips like handles, drilling her from behind as she takes it on all fours.

Her shoulder is fine. She swears. But I keep an eye out for any signs of stress. Though with all the endorphins and oxytocin pumping through our bloodstreams, I'm not sure either of us could feel much pain at this point.

"More," my girl begs, sending a rush through my body, feeding the beast that needs to give her everything I have.

Easy or hard, she'll always get my all.

But in this case, I'm afraid to go harder, driving her upper body forward, forcing her to push back in order to stay upright.

Instead, I lean back, spread my knees, and pull her back as I ram forward. That first slap of contact—her ass to my pelvis—has us both moaning.

Fuck, that's good.

Slap after slap, the sounds and smell of sex fill the room, turning on all my senses. The need to consume her, own her, claim her, rages through me. That primal part of myself I've kept closed off. Holding back, but not really. She knows me. All of me. It's just this baser side is all action mixed with heightened emotional need to own and be owned.

"Who do you belong to, Daisy?" I almost don't recognize the deepness of my voice. *Almost.*

Goosebumps erupt across her flawless skin, though my eyes land on her scar below her shoulder.

"You," she screams.

She's close.

"Who do I belong to?"

"Me?"

I slap her ass. "Is that a question?"

"Ah! No. You belong to me," she cries.

"That's right." I slap the other cheek, watching it redden. "Don't forget that. Only yours."

Her legs start to shake as a pink flush races up her limbs. "Reid."

"I got you." *I've always got you.*

The first instinct is to go faster, but what my girl needs is steady stokes, hitting the same spots over and over again. Only fumbling idiots change their pace or stroke when they've found the sweet spot.

When she says *more,* she means more of the same. But sometimes she does mean more, harder. It's all about reading her reactions and the shaking of her limbs, her moans, her breathing, her straining, pushing, squeezing me—all signs she's nearly there.

I knead and grip her hips and ass, spreading her, increasing the tension, maximizing contact with each slap, each thrust, each glorious squeeze on my cock.

"You drive me crazy, Wildflower. So hot and wet. Your greedy cunt squeezing me, sucking me back in each time, stealing pleasure and giving it back."

"Reid," she moans.

"That's it. Come for me, suck the life out of my cock."

"Ohmygod!" she cries as she comes so fucking hard, her legs give out.

I hold her by her hips, drilling through her spasms. I hold off as long as I can, but her grip on my cock is too good to resist. As I spill inside her, I reach around and pinch her clit, lock on her neck and suck until she comes again.

Finally sated and limp from loving my woman, I fall to my back, pulling her into my side, mumbling, "Love you, Flower."

All is right with the world when she breathes into my neck, "Love you right back," before we drift off.

CHAPTER 17

I PRACTICALLY CRAWL OUT OF BED. EVERY MUSCLE aches with overuse. I make it to the bathroom before Reid even notices I'm gone. That man is insatiable. You'd think my girly parts were made of chocolate, and he's a chocaholic. Not complaining, just need an activity today that doesn't include his massive cock inside my tenderness. Though, being loved by him is worth—

I catch my reflection in the mirror. My left breast has red, circular marks from his fingertips clenching it during our second go-around—as he came. It was hot. So hot.

Scanning, I find more marks on my hips, also from his fingers, but the mark on the side of my neck is from his mouth.

He gave me a hickey. What am I, sixteen?

I look well used and well loved, and that does something to my insides. It settles the unease, the guilt, the uncertainty of being enough, of being what he needs. By the looks of me, I'd say I'm exactly what he needs.

The idea that I'm enough circles on repeat as I shower, coming to terms with the fact that he came to bring me home. But home to where? I no longer have one. If I go—who am I kidding? *When* I go—I'll be homeless and jobless.

I'll have *him*. Anything after that is a bonus.

"Daisy?" The timbre of his morning voice breaches my watery solitude as the shower door opens and in steps my Sequoia, too big for such a confined space. "You snuck…" his words fall away. His brow puckers as he reaches, pulling me closer. "Flower." His remorse fills his nickname for me—the one I love.

"Don't." I rise to my tiptoes, cupping his cheek. Pressing against him, I hide his marks. But it's not enough; his gaze follows his thumb as he rubs the spot on the neck. "I love it. Every moment."

"I hurt you."

"I don't feel hurt. I feel wanted."

His eyes flash to mine, and his nostrils flare. His grip on my waist ensures I don't move—can't move. "You like it?"

Wrapping my arms round his neck, I press in impossibly closer. "I love it. Except maybe the spot on my neck. That'll be hard to hide."

"You're mine," he growls like the last thing he wants is for me to hide any of his marks, even though he's torn between feeling bad and caveman pride for showing the world I belong to him.

"I am, and I'm not ashamed that I'm yours. I won't cover it if you'd rather I didn't." I really don't care, other than Sage and Dad might give me an interesting glance or two.

But if it makes Reid happy, how easy is it to do nothing and wear his marks proudly? Easy. So very easy.

He presses his mouth to the spot on my neck, licking and gently biting. "I might have to keep replacing this one when it fades."

I shudder at the thought. "I could tattoo *Reid's* on my neck. If that would make you feel better." I'm teasing, of course, until his grip on me tightens and his length hardens between us.

"Don't tease." His hands traverse lower, kneading my butt, separating my cheeks and teasing his fingers along my sensitive parts that want nothing more than his adoration all over again.

I bite his shoulder as he hikes my leg up, slipping his thoroughly naughty fingers inside me, pumping slowly. "Reid," I sigh, holding tighter as goosebumps erupt.

"Are you sore?" He nudges my face with his, encouraging me to look at him. "Truth," he commands.

Which I don't want to give. "Kiss me," I offer instead.

He swoops in for a searing kiss, continuing to pump his fingers as I grind against him. "Don't stop," I plead, wanting this so, so much, but then I also want his cock, his tongue.

As I near the edge, he breaks our kiss, trailing his mouth down my neck, his free hand caressing everywhere he can reach. "Are you sore from my cock, Wildflower? Can you take more?"

I clench around him.

"Fuck." He nips at my neck. "I almost don't care. But tell me, before I do something stupid."

"Like fuck me?"

"Jesus, Daisy. You can't say that if you're sore. I won't hurt you."

I run my fingers through the back of his hair, locking on a handful, tugging gently to get his attention. When his brown eyes land on my greens, I give him the only truth he needs, "Make it hurt, Reid. Show me how much you want me."

The fierceness of his features softens as his forehead lands on mine. "Daisy, I don't need to hurt you to show you my love—my want. I'm not about that. I was rough with you last night. Today, I want to make love, not fuck."

"But what if I want—"

"Who's in charge, Flower?"

OhmyholyGrandmaJean. My fierce Sequoia is back. I swallow through my surging want. "You."

"That's right, baby. Your pleasure is my pleasure. I'll give you what you need, how you need it. You'll take my cock the way I give it and come when I say."

Yes, sir is on the tip of my tongue. But that's not what this is—it's not what we are. He's giving me exactly what I need. To know he needs me. He's got me. "Reid?"

He kisses my nose. "Yeah, Daisy?"

"I need to come." I've been hanging on the edge for so long, my legs are weak and shaky.

"Yeah, you do." He backs me up to the warm shower tiles, lifting me as he goes.

My back hits the wall, and he slams home, stealing my breath in one second, crying out the next as my sensitive insides adjust to his size.

Frowning, he tips my chin. "You are sore."

"A little. But I'm good. I want this. I want you."

"My girl," he breathes into our barely there kiss.

And I want to raise a flag that says *I'm his girl*, wear a t-shirt, and put a sign on my car.

My Sequoia.

His pumps are slow and meticulous, our endless kiss, languid and luscious.

Pinned by his hips, his gaze slides to where we're joined, where he's filling me deliciously slowly. The sight is too much. My head falls back, moaning my approval, my want, my desire for him to fill me with everything he has.

His head follows mine, his mouth teasing my neck as he starts to rub my clit. "Want to feel you come on my cock before we both go together."

Ohmy... That's not going to take long.

Slow and steady, he fills me over and over. With each thrust, my need for him grows as if I could possibly want him more. Apparently I can because I'm ravenous for him.

Deep and salaciously gruff, he whispers dirtiness in my ear.

Two times he makes me come before he quickens his pace and gives me the hardness I crave *from him*, sending me into another tailspin before he whispers, "Flower," across my lips as he comes deep inside me, intensifying the last of my quaking pleasure he so perfectly pulls from me time and time again.

CHAPTER 18

I WATCH MY GIRL AS SHE SETS THE TABLE, leaving me to make breakfast. Pancakes. I know she loves them, and it's one of my specialties. I was surprised she had the ingredients, as if she was hoping I'd show up to make them. Maybe subconsciously she was. Kinda wish she could create one of her smoothies to go along with breakfast, but I'd rather dote on her today. She earned it last night.

"Can I help?" She pops a hip, leaning on the counter next to me.

The dirty thoughts that race to the tip of my tongue are swallowed as I offer, "You want to flip? Or finish the eggs?"

"Eggs," she answers too quickly, moving to scoot around me to the other side of the stove where I'm scrambling the eggs.

I catch her waist, slide her in front of me, and hold her in place with a gentle grip on her hip. "Let me show you." I slip the spatula under the first pancake, lift and quickly flip it. "See? Not so tough." I hand her the spatula. "You try."

"How do you know when they're ready to flip?"

I point to the bubbles along the top. "See how the batter firms up on the edges, and bubbles start to form? When that happens, it's ready. Just slide, lift, flip—quickly." I stand back, giving her space.

Tentatively she asks, "You sure you don't want to do it?"

Placing my hand on her back, I kiss her freshly washed hair. "I'm sure. If you mess up, it doesn't matter. It's just food. It'll look worse where it's going." I work on the eggs, only partially watching.

That seems to settle her. She gets right in there and flips it perfectly to land in the same place. Then she does the next two without me asking.

"You're a natural."

She kisses my jaw. "I had a good teacher."

Damn, she's sweet. I hate to damn the moment, but we have things to discuss, and if she's going to be mad at me, I'd like to have the whole day to make it up to her. "Can we talk about my mom?"

She hesitates only for a second before nodding.

"At first, I didn't know she knew you. That you already had a relationship with her through your shop. When I found out she was trying to set us up, I asked her to stop. I didn't need or want her help—I had already started buying flowers from you on Tuesdays. Then when we started dating, I didn't want anyone else in that relationship but us—especially not my family, who have way too many opinions on my love life as it is. We were new and important to me. It felt like our relationship was in the works for so long. I didn't want to set us back by bringing in my family—my mom and sister—to jinx it. You only met my brothers out of necessity."

She frowns. "You didn't want me to meet your family?"

"Not the way you did. I wanted you comfortable with me—with us—before you were swallowed up by my overly invested and overwhelming family. You'd think everyone was in committed relationships besides me, but that's not the case. I didn't date much. Didn't have much interest—till I saw you. Once they figured out I liked you, they hounded me incessantly about asking you out. I wanted a chance for you to fall in love with me before falling for them."

"They are pretty incredible. Would you have ever asked me out if it wasn't for the flooding in my basement?"

I turn off the stove, remove the pancakes, and pull her into my arms. "Without a doubt. I'm a little slow in getting started, but once I do, I'm full force."

She laughs. "Yeah, I've noticed, Mr. I'm In Charge."

"Hey—" I squeeze her ass. "You like my bossy. It gets you hot." Does it ever. She was melting in my hands in the shower.

"Yeah, it does," she wispily admits, a slight flush pinkening her cheeks.

"Me too." I kiss the center of each cheek, squeezing her ass

123

and groaning when my body starts to react to my beautiful Flower. We need to eat before I devour her instead of the food. "Let's eat."

After a few bites, she studies me for a moment before asking, "So when would you have told me about your mom?"

"I was planning on telling you the night of the fire during our date. But you finished with the wedding early and then the shower, and what happened during and afterwards. It didn't seem like the right time."

"I can see that. Any other secrets or information you're holding back I should know about?"

"Nope." I point to her food. "Eat. Then I'm taking you out."

"I think we should go to the beach."

"Really?"

"Yeah, I haven't gone since I've been here."

Surely she's had time. "Why not."

She shrugs.

"Daisy," I use my *Mr. I'm In Charge* voice.

"I've been sad, okay? I didn't do much besides cry over you and work—well, and heal."

I grip her hand. "Are you okay? Are we okay?"

Her smile is brighter than the sun. "I haven't felt this happy in—ever."

Good. I want to keep that smile in place as much as possible. I know we'll have rocky times—highs and lows—but... "As long as we have each other, we'll get through the good and the bad. I promise."

She nods as she forks a bite. "You need to officially meet

124

Sage and then my dad." She doesn't seem too thrilled with that prospect.

"I'm happy to meet whoever you want as long as you're by my side."

"I think I can live with that." She flinches when she realizes what she said.

I grip the back of her neck. "You are my life, Daisy. Not letting go. Not then. Not now."

She nods, swiping at an errant tear. "Same."

Sage is drunk as he animatedly tells Reid about nearly getting bitten by a shark. Each time he tells it, his encounter gets more perilous, especially the more he drinks. I think it was a five-foot shark when I heard the story the first time. Now, it's as large as a boat by the span of his hands trying to estimate the size of the shark's jaw.

"You like him." Dad offers me a bottled water, his eyes on Reid.

"I love him." Plain and simple. Though it seems anything but plain or simple. It's deep and cavernous, haunting, and humbling how much I love him and he loves me. He fills up my darkness with light and his gruff ways.

"I think the feeling is mutual." Dad glances at me before returning to Sage and Reid.

"He loves me, Daddy."

He nods, soaking that in. A moment passes before he adds, "You're leaving."

"Yeah, tomorrow or the next day." I think after last night and a full day at the beach, and now a cookout, I just want to sleep tomorrow, not do anything but relax in my Sequoia's arms instead of leaving right away and being separated by driving our own cars.

"We'll miss you, but he obviously makes you happy. He seems to be a good man."

"He is. The best. And, yeah, he makes me scary happy."

Dad kisses my temple, a tender move he's only done a few times in my life. "Don't be scared, Daisy. Love is magical and wonderous. Soak it up. Let it take you away."

Dad has never been so forthcoming or open about love or his opinion of it. I thought he was just a womanizer who followed his libido. Maybe he's following love where he can find it.

"What will you do?" he asks.

"I think I'll see if I can work for his mom. She owns the flower market where the local florists buy all their goods. We've become friends over the years."

"You should do something with your art."

"What art?" Reid slips his arm around my waist, pulling me against his chest.

Dad pats him on the shoulder. "Check the guest bedroom." Then he walks off, stopping a few feet away. "Don't leave without saying goodbye to me and the guys."

I assume he means leaving town. I've only left town once, and it was to move to Round Rock, Reid's hometown. I didn't leave then without saying goodbye. I've no intention of leaving now without doing it either.

Dad's projecting. Sage and I are the only ones with family morals. Leaving without saying goodbye is Dad and Mom's history. Not mine. "Okay. But we're going to head in now, I think."

Dad raises his beer to us. "Night."

"Your dad and brother are nice." Reid kisses my shoulder.

Yeah, they are, most of the time. I'm ready to go and figure out the rest of our life. "Can we do nothing tomorrow and leave the day after?"

"You sure? We can stay the rest of the week."

I grip his hand and pull him toward the path home. "I'm ready to go home. But I need a day of rest first. Someone wore me out last night and today."

He releases my hand, putting his arm around my waist, then dropping it lower to squeeze my ass. "I need a taste, Flower. Then you can sleep the day away."

"A taste?"

"Your pussy, Daisy. I'm going to eat your pussy for dessert." He squeezes again. "Maybe breakfast too."

Yes, please. "I'm gonna need a shower first. I've got sand where there shouldn't be any."

He chuckles. "Yeah, I've got a few grains in uncomfortable places myself."

CHAPTER 19

AS REID SHOWERS, I WAIT ON THE BED, then decide that's too obvious—too needy, too desperate. I slip on one of his t-shirts and get us some waters. As I turn the corner, Reid is just coming out of the bathroom, droplets glistening on this tanned skin as he walks straight into the bedroom. Seconds later he returns to the hall, finding me stuck on the vision of him walking out in only a towel, determination in his stride.

"There you are." His relief brings a smile to my lips. Did he think I'd disappear on him? Looking like *that*?

"Looking for me?" I ask as if I had time to dress and leave. I think he took a quicker shower than me.

He eats up the distance between us in a few long strides, taking in the glasses of water—one in each hand—and his shirt I donned. "I'm looking for my dessert."

Would that be me?

He said it was, but what if he was just teasing, trying to turn me on without actually following through? No, that's not who Reid is. He doesn't make false promises, and he follows through. He's a finisher. He said so himself.

I've felt it myself.

"Here I am." I nearly choke on the words. Sexual confidence is a hard one for me until he turns me on so much, I'll ride him with abandon.

"Damn, bold looks good on you." His smoldering sexuality jumps a notch or two as he stops in front of me, taking the glasses, setting them down on the coffee table, and lifting me to wrap my legs around his middle. He grips the back of my hair, pressing his mouth to mine. The kiss is tender and teasing of promises to come.

I hold around his shoulders, trying to get closer, trying to eat him alive as his free hand kneads my ass, finding me pantyless and already wet.

Always wet for him. It would be embarrassing if it didn't turn him on in return.

"Now, do I want my dessert in here or the bedroom?" He quirks a brow, waiting for my reply.

"Um, bedroom?" Yeah, my sexual confidence only goes so far. If he wants his mouth on me, I'll take it any way—anywhere—he's willing to do it. But the bed sounds more comfortable.

He nods but moves to the kitchen table, kicking out a chair and setting me on the edge of the cool wood surface. "I think my girl needs to know I'll eat her anywhere, anytime."

Ohmyholy—

He sits, pushing my legs open, scooting forward. Starting at my feet, he runs his fingertips up my legs, his eyes never leaving mine. "T-shirt off, Flower."

I comply before I consider the brightness of the room and the fact I'm on full display.

He takes the shirt, folding it into a square and standing. With a hand across the top of my chest, he gently pushes. "Lie back."

I hold on to his wrist, using the support to slow my descent.

"Lift." He places the folded shirt below my head when I rise up. His eyes trail over my face, over my breasts, down my abdomen, to my center before returning to me. "You're so fucking beautiful, Daisy, laid out ready to take whatever I give. Or give whatever I want to take."

I feel beautiful in his eyes.

He leans over, gripping the front of my neck, giving it a gentle squeeze. "Don't doubt that I want you in every way imaginable." His hands move lower to squeeze and tease my nipples. "I want to make you come in so many ways." His eyes lock on my nipples as he pinches, then kneads my breasts. "It's almost indecent how often I think about it now that I have you back."

My center floods as I squirm, needing him, needing more.

"Be still, baby." He plumps my breasts, flicking his tongue over each before kissing and licking lower, taking his time, twisting my nipples a few more times before he runs his hands down my sides, his rough fingertips leaving a trail of goosebumps.

Lower.

Lower.

"Reid." I'm a begging mess by the time he sits and runs kisses up each thigh, avoiding my core, teasing me all the more.

"Patience, Flower. My timing. Your pleasure." He caresses the apex of my thighs.

I try to be still, but it's hard. Everything in me wants him on me, in me. I grab my breast and squeeze, needing the contact, the release.

"Fuck that's hot." His eyes meet mine over my mound where he takes a lungful of my scent and groans his approval.

I close my eyes and gasp in embarrassment.

"Don't," he warns. "I love your smells. I've no doubt I'll love your taste even more." He kisses the inside of my thigh.

It's a tender gesture compared to his command. "But you haven't—"

"I am, baby." Slowly he runs his fingers along my seam, teasing my entrance then up to my clit, blowing softly. He lifts my legs over his shoulders. "Let your knees fall open."

OhmyholyGrandmaJean. Kill me now.

He helps me do as instructed with a grip on my thighs.

On a feral groan, he kisses me intimately with tongue, delving in, licking, sucking, stealing my breath.

Finally, finally, I scream in my head as I arch back, coming off the table.

"Still," he reprimands, holding me down with a hand across my abdomen.

He's insane if he thinks I can remain still. "I can't," I moan. He may want it. He may demand it, but it doesn't mean I'll comply, that I can.

When he runs the hand holding me down up to my breasts, teasing my nipple at the same time he begins to lick and suck on my clit, I know I'm done for. I won't last.

He groans his approval, the louder I moan and rock my hips, trying to ride his face. My mind is filled with visions of him devouring me at the same time as shoving his cock inside me.

"Reid!" I scream when he fills me with his fingers, rubbing, taunting my G-spot like the expert lover he is.

How many? How many women has he made come like this? Did they survive? Did they follow him around town like a puppy begging for scraps—for more?

Because I will be front of the line, begging for him to do this again on endless repeat. "Please don't stop."

He growls his agreement into my body, no words needed.

The second I think of sucking his cock like my pussy wants to suck him in, I start to shake and tremble, my orgasm nearing, moisture pooling.

His grip on me tightens, his command clear. *Come.* His silent bark shudders through my body.

Seconds later I'm pole-vaulting over the edge of reason, bowing off the table as I scream my release, gripping his hair, holding him in place, afraid he'll stop before I've eked out all the pleasure my orgasm shoots through my limbs, my core, and to my heart. Falling even harder for the man between my legs.

He kisses and lazily licks me till I've returned to my body, limp and hardly able to move.

In slow, even strides, he picks me up and carries me to the bedroom. "Now for the bed."

Ohmy... "Again?"

"Oh, Flower, I've just gotten started."

CHAPTER 20

MY GIRL'S A HEAP OF SATED, WELL-LOVED flesh when I leave her in bed to find a snack. A crisp apple is the first thing I find, and, taking a huge bite, I wander her apartment, truly taking it in. It doesn't have the hominess her own place had, but then, these aren't her things. These are her father's or maybe even her brother's belongings.

I hesitate at the closed door to the guest room that's down from her room and bathroom. I test the knob, and when it turns, I open the door and feel for the light switch on the wall to my right.

The overhead light illuminates, casting shadows around the room but highlighting painting after painting lining the walls— not hung, sitting on the floor, leaning against the wall, side by side. Every inch and then some is covered by my Flower's amazing gift and artful eye.

My heart aches as I picture her here pouring her heart, her grief, her vision into these canvases one stroke at a time. She said she healed in her time here, was this what she meant?

Was she crying? Was she sad? Did she feel better or worse afterwards?

I'm immediately drawn to the one on the easel set close to the window. Bright flames lick at a dark figure emerging from a fire with a woman in his arms. The guy is broad-shouldered, big, territorial, yet his features aren't discernable through the shadows keeping him hidden. She's captured a feeling without actually showing their faces. Remarkable.

Moving back, I study it from other angles. Is this me? Is this how she sees me? Menacing or fireproof? Am I rescuing her or leaving her?

The fire painting is different from the rest, darker. The others are beach scenes with surfers or sunbathers, or flowers. Lots and lots of flowers. Not fields or vases of flowers but individual flowers, like a daisy, tulip, and many others I don't know the names of. They're colorful, detailed, and so realistic.

Amazing. All of it.

My apple done, I take one more look in her room of escape before closing the door. I finish in the kitchen, go to the bathroom and return to my sleeping beauty, who's full of talent and potential, and yet she's been here in her father's garage apartment hiding away.

She needs to come home, let me help her find her way.

"Fuuuck," he groans, gripping my hair, his head thrown back, the muscles in his abdomen flexing and straining. It only turns me on more, making me ravenous for his pleasure.

Fall apart for me, I silently plead, praying what I have to give is what he needs. I know he's enjoying it, the hardness in his length is proof enough. But does my touch, my desire, my love hit the right notes?

Do I feed his soul like he does mine?

Do I tap the beast in him and drain him dry?

Or is he still holding back?

As I suck him long and deep, faster and faster, he fills the air with his grunts and endless stream of colorful curses and dirty requests.

This is not the man I once thought had little to say. He has so much—

"Baby, stop teasing." It's not a command. He doesn't force his cock down my throat. He doesn't take the pleasure I know he wants, but right now I want him to.

"Fuck my mouth." I barely take a breath before looking up, offering, "Take what you need."

He stills. Looking down, he runs his thumb along my cheek before gripping my hair to keep me in place as he pulls back, letting his cock fall from my mouth. "You're perfect."

That's not true. If I were perfect, he would have come by now. "Then take control."

He bends, swiping at my slobbery lips, getting in my face. The feral in his eyes sends tremors through me. He's holding back, yet he's right there ready to show me. "Is that what you need, or is that what you think *I* need?"

I grip his wrist with a tight hold on my hair. "Isn't it what we both need?"

"Jesus, Flower." He closes his eyes and takes a steadying breath, then stands. He rubs my jaw. "Open, tongue out."

I shudder, anxious for everything he's going to set free. I open my mouth, sticking out my tongue.

Holding the base of his cock, he flicks it up and down, slapping my tongue a few times. "You want my cock, Daisy?"

"Yes." I'm desperate for him.

"Where, baby?" He slides the tip in just enough to pass my lips, then pulls out.

I contemplate for a second too long, lost in the sight of him in all his sexual glory.

He bends down again. "You need to tell me where you want my cock."

Is this a trick question?

I'm giving him a blow job. Or, I was.

Does he not want more?

I am bad at it?

Is it more than the blow job?

Am *I* not enough?

Tears prick the back of my eyes at the possibility. I fall back on my haunches.

He releases his grip on my hair. "What just happened?"

I avert my gaze, looking down at my naked body, feeling too exposed and vulnerable. I wrap my arm across my breasts. My pulse beats in my ears as my anxiety rises.

He won't let go.

He doesn't trust me.

He wants me but not enough.

"Nothing." I slide away and get to my feet, turning away. We've waited so long to be together. He's here. We've had sex. But it's not enough. *I'm* not enough. Maybe he needs time to trust I won't leave him again. "Let's go home."

"Daisy." He tugs me back to him by my wrist. I don't fight. I've lost my fight. He cups my cheek, trying to lock gazes, but I close my eyes. "What's going on in that beautiful head of yours?"

I'm not enough. It's on the tip of my tongue, but I know him. He'll argue I'm exactly what he needs, yet he'll hold back, not let go, not fully.

We're new at being intimate with each other. Maybe he needs time.

It still hurts.

"I'm going to pack." I pull away, and he lets me. "I'll be ready in an hour."

"Daisy."

I ignore the pain in his voice. "If you can't wait, I understand. I have my car. I can call you when I get to town." *I can find a place to stay if you don't want me with you.*

What am I doing? Just talk to him.

"I thought you wanted to rest today." He follows me to the bedroom, watching as I slip on clothes.

I shrug. "I'm either going, or I'm not. There's no point in waiting."

"Hey." He bands around me from behind, his arms across my chest and waist. "Tell me what happened."

I have. He doesn't hear me. "Can we talk about it later please?" *As in never.*

"I'm holding you to that." He releases me with a kiss to my head. "I'm going to grab a shower."

"Yep." I was so excited to go home. Now, I'm doubting if it's the right thing to do, but the reality is things won't get better if we're apart. If he's in Round Rock, then I need to be there too. Otherwise, I might as well break things off. I fall on the bed and succumb to tears at the thought.

I don't want to let him go.

So why the hell did I pull away—shut him down?

Why couldn't I have just answered him and let him fuck me however he wanted? We'd be cuddling on the couch or bed by now. Instead, I'm crying on my own, and he's probably jerking off in the shower because I left him hanging.

I've made a mess of things.

How do I come back from this? If he pushed, took what he wanted, I wouldn't be all knotted up inside. Now, I don't know how to unwind. How to stop the worry and make it right.

The chasm between what he wants and what I can give

D.M. DAVIS

grows exponentially in the time it takes me to pack and load my car.

With quick goodbyes to my family and the guys at the surf shop, we start off for home.

Him in his car.

And me in mine.

Distance. It's visceral, like an uninvited third party between us.

140

CHAPTER 21

I DON'T KNOW WHAT THE FUCK HAPPENED back there. One second, she's sucking my cock, driving me insane, and the next she's teary-eyed and closed off.

I didn't push.

I'm starting to think I should have. Taking control turns her on, but this is more than sex, and I don't want to steamroll her with what I think she needs, but it's important we actually communicate feelings. She needs to tell me, and today she couldn't because she's still holding back.

Doubt creeps in. Am I holding back too?

She's definitely the one holding back.

She didn't want to come first the other day because she felt she needed to be punished for leaving, for not believing in us enough to fight through the ugliness of the fire and the lie of omission of who Mary is to me.

Before I can think twice, I call her.

"Hey." Her defeated greeting confirms I'm doing the right thing.

"Pull over." It's not a command, but I don't leave room for deliberation.

"Where?" I can imagine her looking around for a place to stop.

I recall a sign a ways back. "There's a rest stop in one mile. Pull in and park."

"O-okay."

When we hit the rest stop, she turns in and drives past the restroom area to a shaded spot near the exit. I hop out as soon as I put my truck in park. Daisy doesn't get out, which is concerning, but then she has no idea why I asked her to stop. For all she knows, I needed to piss.

Coming around the front of her car so she sees me, I spot her blowing her nose and wiping at her face. It guts me that she's been crying in her car as I followed behind, completely unaware of how upset she is.

I open her door and offer my hand. She unbuckles, slips her hand in mine, and steps out. I continue to hold her hand as we walk away from the parking lot, looking for a place with a little privacy away from prying eyes. We come to an area with benches and tables, but many are occupied with families eating lunch or taking a break from the road. We continue down a path through trees that open to an outcropping with a view of the ocean.

I halt and turn, jarring her to a stop seconds before she bumps into me. I release her hand and close the distance between us. Her gaze meets mine as I lean down, brushing my lips across hers, barely pressing forward, whispering, "I love you, Flower. If you're hurting, I'm hurting."

Tears well in her green eyes and start trickling down her cheeks. "I'm sorry—"

"Baby—" I cup her cheeks, brushing at her tears. "No apologies. It's okay. I just need you to talk to me when you feel like this. Don't shut me out."

She nods, wrapping her arms around my middle, laying her head on my chest and hugging me tightly. "I don't know what that was. I wanted you to come, to enjoy yourself. I wanted you to let go, not hold back. But then—" She hiccups and cries harder. "I feel…" She takes a stunted breath. "Like I'm not enough."

"Daisy." She's breaking my heart. I pick her up, walk a few paces to a rock ledge and sit with her across my lap. "You're perfect for me. I don't want you any other way. I swear. I'm not holding back."

"But you like it h-haard."

Jesus. Looking up, I scrub my face with my free hand. *She's killing me.*

I tip her chin till our eyes meet. "You need to hear me. Are you listening?"

She nods.

"I love it hard. I love it gentle. I love eating you, filling you,

143

making you come. I love it all—with *you*." I squeeze her chin to keep her focus. "Let me say that again. *With. You.* Whatever I may have liked in the past doesn't even come into play with you. I'm so fucking gone for you, Wildflower, every time with you is the *best* I've ever had."

"Really?"

I press my forehead to hers. "Really. Best. Ever."

She lets out a long breath, and her shoulders drop. "Me too. Blow-my-mind good."

Thank the heavens.

"Then do us both a favor, stop overthinking it. If you start having doubts, you stop and tell me. I'll set you straight. I'll make you come so hard you can't even remember you were ever even worried."

"Okay." She stands, shaking out her limbs, cracking her neck and wiping the last of the moisture from her face. "I'm sorry. I should have just told you what was going on. Forgive me?"

"Forgiven." I stand and kiss her brow, lightly gripping her neck. "Now, when we get home? I'm coming down your throat so fucking hard, you'll be tasting me for a week."

She shudders. "Yes, please."

Good girl is on the tip of my tongue. But I'm not a Dom, and she's not my sub. She's my equal in life and in the bedroom. I may like control, but I mainly just want to control her pleasure and give her more and more and more.

"Let's hit the bathrooms and then hit the road."

"I'd like to stop for lunch soon."

I assume she's not offering herself for lunch. She's a savory treat I only want in private, not in the open, not where she can be seen. What we have is for my eyes—our eyes only. It's real—not a show. "Sounds like a plan."

After sharing a soft, slow kiss, we head back the way we came, our steps lighter than before.

Any hope of loving on my Flower when we got home flies by the wayside as soon as we pull up to my home. My family is standing on the doorstep, arms loaded with what I assume is a feast. I called and told Mom we were almost home. I didn't anticipate them sneakily banding together to welcome us—welcome *her*.

I should have suspected when Mom wanted an estimated time of arrival. Thankfully, we were late rather than early, otherwise, they would have gotten an earful of me pleasing my girl.

I glance at Daisy seconds before she exits her car, tears already streaming down her cheeks as Mom rushes down the stairs, heading right for her. Their embrace is heartfelt and full of more tears. I suppose, circumstances aside, I'm lucky my girl and my mom already know and care about each other. Makes the integration already feel natural.

"Hey, man. Welcome home." Galant opens my door.

"Hey." I pry my eyes from my mom and girlfriend having a moment to greet the rest of my family.

Galant and Turner grab our bags with *hellos* to Daisy as they pass. Dad stands on the porch, keeping sentry, waiting on Mom to find forgiveness I know has been eating at her since the night

145

of the fire when Daisy discovered our connection at the worst possible moment.

I wave to him as I step up to my girl and Mom and join their hug, kissing them on the heads and then leaving them to make up in their time, with privacy.

"You doing okay?" I offer my hand to Dad.

He swats it away, gripping me in a rough hug. "What, too old for a hug from your old man?" His voice is gruff from years of smoking before he gave it up.

"Nope. Never too old for a hug."

"Glad you two are home. Your mom has been fretting." His eyes land on Mom.

"Glad to be here, but y'all can't stay long. I need—"

"Time alone. I got it. I'll round everyone out after we eat." He squeezes my shoulder, urging me through the front door. "They'll be in when they're ready. Let's give them a bit of peace."

One final glance over my shoulder and I close the door behind me.

CHAPTER 22

"OH, DAISY. I'M SO SORRY. PLEASE CAN YOU ever forgive me? What can I do to make things right between us?" she cries into our hug.

"You were right. He's a wonderful man." My tears match hers. "I forgive you. Reid explained it all. We're good."

Honestly, I probably wouldn't have reacted very well whenever I found out, since neither of them knew that I knew the other one initially. It's not like Reid could have come in my store and said, *"You know my mom, Mary. Blah, blah, blah."* That would have been the best, but he didn't know.

His mom also didn't know he had started to come see me after she started trying to set me up with her youngest son. Though, initially, she was offering any of her sons, just trying to get me to bite.

It felt nice to be cared about, but I wasn't interested in her sons. I already had my eyes on my Sequoia. Hoping someday he'd see me.

Turns out he saw me all along.

I should have accepted her blind date set-up!

Pulling back, I dry my face with my sleeves, really looking around for the first time. "Isn't this your farm?"

Mary sniffles and nods. "Yes. Reid moved in here after the fire at your place so we could watch after him. He's hoping you'll like it and want to make it your home too."

I blink at her, not knowing what to say. Reid and I haven't discussed it.

She bumps me with her shoulder as we face his home. "It was our original house before we built farther up on the ridge. Though some days I do miss this view by the pond." She sighs, looking at the house where a large figure stands at the window, staring back as us. "He didn't tell you, did he?"

"No, but in all fairness, we've had a lot to talk though. Poor guy, I've been really lonely since I moved. He's kinda had to deal with my emotional baggage these last few days."

Hugging me again, she whispers, "It's good for him. He's a good listener. Always has been." She releases me but squeezes my shoulders. "He loves you, Daisy. Don't doubt that. That boy has been miserable without you."

Her words pick at my guilt. I did that to him—to us. But

it's nice to hear that his mom knows how much he cares about me and us. "Same."

The front door opens, and Reid steps out. "Mom, I'd like to talk to Daisy, if you don't mind."

She winks at me then heads toward him. "I don't mind. Don't take long. Food's getting cold."

He waits until she closes the door before stepping down, offering me his hand. "Walk with me?"

"Sure."

He seems somber, watching his feet and then the hillside as we trek the incline. "I have a feeling Mom already told you my plan." He side-eyes me as we come to a stop at the top of the hill that offers a view of their farm and the fields of flowers below.

"I don't know. What's your plan?"

"I'd like us to live here. Get married when you're ready. Fix up the house. We could even build in a few years if you're happy here but need more room." His eyes flit to my stomach.

Is he thinking about kids? My insides do a little flip at the thought of having a forever with him—a forever that includes children and grandbabies, hopefully even great-grandbabies.

"If not, we can find something closer to town." He grips my waist, holding me to him. "Wherever you're happy is where I want to be."

I place my hands on his chest, looking up into the face of the man who makes my heart sing and my dreams take root. "What do you want?"

He takes my hand as we walk the ridge heading to a field beyond the flowers to our left and the pond and his house below. "I'd like to live here. Raise a family with you. Work the farm. You can paint or work with Mom at the Flower Mart or do whatever you want. I just want you, Daisy. Really, it's that simple."

"But you're a firefighter."

He nods, looking at our joined hands, and swallows before meeting my eyes. "I'm not sure I want to be one anymore. I've had a couple of scares, and I'll be honest, I don't want to put you through that. Plus, it's physically taxing, makes us old before our time, high risks of breathing problems. I'm in my prime, and I want to stay that way for you," he runs his hand along my lower abdomen, "for our kids." He runs his lips across my brow. "But even more, I don't want to risk my life, risk our future when I don't love it enough anymore."

Wow. He's really thought about this. "You don't?"

He shakes his head, turning us to start back. "I thought I did until—"

"That night I brought you tacos and you held me all night."

He smiles as if he savors the memory as much as me. "Yeah, the fire was out of control that night. We were lucky to get out without any injuries." He stops to face me, cupping my cheek. "It was the first time I had something to lose—" his voice cracks, and his eyes begin to water.

"Reid." I lean up, pulling his head down to mine, kissing his cheeks.

One blink and his tears are falling. "You're my world, Wildflower. I don't want a job that puts that in jeopardy. I never really loved it like my brothers, dad, and grandfather. Though, Dad took early retirement. Maybe he feels the same—now."

As much as I love him not putting his life on the line every time he goes to work, I don't want him to feel pressure from me to quit no matter how much it scares me. "Are you still going back?"

"Yeah, this will be my last season. Then I thought I'd work the land and support you in whatever you decide you want to do." He swipes at his face, sniffing, his sadness fading away.

"And if I want to travel the world?"

"I'll pack a bag." He bends down, lifting me by my thighs. Screeching in laugher, I wrap around him as he spins us.

"Where you go, I go, Flower."

"I think I like the sound of that."

"Yeah?" He slows our spin, stopping as his lips connect with mine. "Marry me, Daisy. Let me spend the rest of my life making you happy—" he sucks my bottom lip, "—making you come."

OhmyholyGrandmaJean. "Who can turn down a proposal like that?"

"Is that a *yes*?"

"Yes, my giant Sequoia. I'll marry you, live here with you, give you babies, work the farm with you, work with your mom—if she'll have me, and spend the rest of my life making you happy." I devour his lips for a few short seconds before adding, "Making you come."

"Jesus, Flower." He squeezes my ass, grinding me against

the hardness in his jeans. "Sounds like the most amazing life ever."

"Sounds like a dream." I grip him tighter, not wanting him to put me down.

"Our dream," he all but breathes into my mouth as he kisses me from the top of the hill to our front porch, only setting me down to pant across my face, "Love you, Daisy."

"Love you back."

"I nearly forgot." He reaches in his pocket and slips a perfect ring on my finger.

"You—" My eyes land on the round diamond on my left hand. "How... you—"

He laughs, running his hand up my arm to capture the back of my neck. "You thought I was gonna come out to get you from your dad's and not have a plan? I was going to propose tonight, but—"

"I ruined it."

"No. You brought us home, where it should have happened in the first place. This is our house until we're busting at the seams. Then I'll build you a new home. Like my dad did for my mom." He keeps me from replying with a mind-numbing kiss that has my head swimming.

"Come on. They're waiting." He squeezes my ass and pushes me through the front door as he opens it. "You're going to have to stand in front of me until my cock calms down. But later—"

I whisper over my shoulder, "I know. You're coming down my throat."

He growls, plastering his front to my back as he wraps his arms around me, slamming his mouth to mine.

A throat clears.

We break apart, catching his dad in the kitchen doorway. "Food's getting cold."

"I think they're hot enough, they'll warm it up from there." Turner chuckles, talking over Dad's shoulder.

Reid guides me forward, still stuck to my back, his hardness too evident to miss. "She said *yes*."

The room erupts with whoops, hollers, and congratulations.

CHAPTER 23

I T'S BEEN TWO WEEKS SINCE I CAME HOME with Reid, agreed to be his wife, and moved in with him. He has another week before he's supposed to go back to work at the firehouse. I can feel his uncertainty if he should even return or resign now. He's torn because the firehouse relies on him, and he hasn't told his family of his plans.

I don't think they'll be disappointed in him. It's obvious how much they love him and want us to be happy in whatever form that takes, but he has to tell them on his timeline.

Currently, he and his dad are redoing our bathroom. Thankfully, the first thing they replaced was the toilet, which was not their original intent. I told him he cannot expect me to live in a house with no toilet for days. He promptly installed the new one, and they graciously vacate whenever I need to use it. It was embarrassing at first, but really, we all do it, so it's no big deal now. It'll be nice to have a shower in our house again instead of driving to his parents' house to use theirs.

Next will be the kitchen, but I'm wondering if we should add another bathroom instead. It's a three-bedroom house. One bathroom isn't enough. But maybe it's best to save that money and start dreaming what our forever house will include when we start building in a few years or so. I kinda like where we are. It's cozy and has history. I also don't mind bumping into my Sequoia as we navigate the small bathroom and kitchen. I rather enjoy it, actually.

He's converted one of the guest bedrooms into a painting studio for me, though once I start working for his mom, I don't know when I'll have time to paint. But he was so proud of his gift, I didn't dare squash his joy. He's bent over backward trying to make me feel at home. And I do, but I worry about his happiness. Will he truly be content giving up his career by choice? The one that pulses through his genes, from generations of firefighters. I guess it depends what's next.

"Daisy?" Reid calls from the front porch, scraping off his shoes, but he doesn't come closer than the threshold.

I turn off the kitchen faucet and dry my hands. "I didn't know you'd left." I glance back to the bathroom, where the work continues.

"Galant is installing the tile. Dad will be back tomorrow to grout."

"I didn't even know he was here."

He only smiles. "Get your shoes. I want to take you somewhere."

I'm not one to turn down an adventure, especially with him. "Do I need to change?"

He scans my sundress, his mouth tilting in a mischievous grin. "Only if you want to go naked."

I gasp and laugh, hoping his brother didn't hear that. "Uh, no."

"Hmm, too bad." In the direction of our bathroom, he shouts, "Galant, eat whatever you can find when you get hungry. We're going out for a while."

"Yep, sure thing. Have fun," he calls.

"Should I get him a drink or something?"

"He'll get it. Come on." Reid holds out his hand. He's impatient to be on our way.

I slip on my tennies at the door and take his hand, letting him pull me down the stairs and to his truck.

Once inside, he starts the engine and motions toward the house. "We're going to build a garage around back. Galant is thinking he might like to move in here once we build our new home."

"Really? It would be nice to have more of your family close by."

He squeezes my knee as we head out. "I'm glad you think so."

As we hit a bit of bumpier terrain, he relinquishes his hold on me to steer with two hands. "Mom and Dad have a lot of land. There's room for all of us to build houses here and still plenty of room to expand the farm, if we want."

"Have your own little Ashford compound?"

He chuckles, "Yeah, something like that."

Over the next ridge, about a mile from our home, he stops near a line of large trees like they were put here as a divider or screen. They're not in a straight line but arched and staggered to give them room to grow without crowding.

"When I was a kid, Dad brought us kids here, and we planted saplings." He turns the car off, "Stay put," and hops out.

After opening my door, he unbuckles my seatbelt, lifting me out and carrying me till we're under the largest of the trees. He sets me down, and we turn to face the direction we just came. My hand is locked in his, the trees to our backs, our view of the valley of their beautiful land below.

"There are a few more plots like this with trees on it. For all of us kids to build on, if we want."

My heart skips. "What?!"

He wraps around me from behind. "This will be the site of our new home. We'll break ground in the coming weeks. Progress might be slow until wildfire season passes, as a lot of the crew will be off-duty firemen, but the core of the crew will keep progressing."

I turn, not wanting to take my eyes off the spectacular view but needing to see my Sequoia's face. "You're for real right now?" I know he wouldn't joke about this, but my shock is making it hard to swallow this news. Who gets swept away by an amazing guy, given a home, and then given property to build a new home of your dreams *with* the man of your dreams? "I thought you wanted to wait until we were bursting at the seams in our current home."

"Our house needs a lot of work. It sat empty for too many years with no updates. The modifications we're doing now will suit Galant. He'll help with the new house, and we'll help with upgrading the old one."

Wow. I'm stunned.

"Too fast?" His worry is evident in the crease of his brow and the downturn of his eyes.

"No. Surprised is all. But, yes, yes to all of it." I turn to look out over the land. "I think I'll need a truck too."

He laughs and pulls me back to his pickup. "I was thinking the same thing." He opens the back door, hands me a blanket and pulls out a basket. "I made us a picnic."

I step back, giving him room to maneuver. "You have an actual picnic basket."

He blushes. "The basket is from Mom, but swear the food is all me, except the dessert I bought at the store."

I silly-girl clap. "There's dessert?!"

He kisses my nose and takes my hand. "Yeah, Flower, two choices."

"You mean two desserts." Surely he doesn't expect me to choose.

"Yeah, that's what I meant." Laughing, he guides me to a more secluded spot where the trees overlap, creating a larger space of shade.

Together we spread out the blanket and sit. With the truck's angle and trees, I don't think anyone coming up the dirt road could see us until they were right on top of us.

As he pulls out the food, I contemplate the truck idea. "I have money from the insurance settlement. I could trade my car in for a new one. Will you go with me?"

He beams. "Actually, I have one on order that's supposed to arrive at the dealer tomorrow. We can check it out, and if you don't like it, there's no obligation, you can pick another one."

"You continue to surprise me." I pick at my dress, feeling thankful but inadequate. "You take such good care…"

"Hey." He tips my chin. "You take care of me too—in the ways I need. In the way only you can."

My vision mists. "Really?"

"Daisy." He sighs, pulling me into his lap, food forgotten. "You are my love. My heart only needs you and the way you love me. I don't need a new car. I just got one. And if you didn't need a better vehicle for the farm, I wouldn't have gotten you one. It's a convenience for you and for me. And I won't worry as much if I know you're driving a new truck that's capable of handling these dirt roads and terrain."

"You're building us a house, getting me a truck—"

"What every man *wants* to do for his woman, I'm just lucky enough to be able to do it. Don't let it make you feel unequal in our relationship. You do more for me than you know."

I choose to take his word.

I feel his contentment—his sigh of relief—when he holds me after being away, after working hard with his dad. He needed me after that fire many moons ago. He sought me out, even though I was the one to come to him.

I settle him. I'm his safe place.

And he's mine.

CHAPTER 24

CAN'T STOP WATCHING HER, WANTING HER,
drooling after her as we eat our lunch under the trees that
will surround our future home. She fears she's not enough.
I fear *I'm* not enough. Maybe building her a house and buying
her a truck is overcompensating, but it's also necessity and the
pleasure of seeing how happy it makes her to be taken care
of—it's surprising how satisfying it is to be the one to do it. She
feeds my heart, soul, and the ache in places she fits so perfectly.
I doubted I'd find anything close to what my parents have.
Now, I think we'll surpass them.

She's not lacking.

She's perfect—for me.

The wind picks up, whipping her long wavy hair in all directions. She fights to keep it out of her mouth as she draws it into her hand at the nape of her neck, frowning.

I reach in my pocket and hold out a band. "Here."

She eyes it like it might bite her. "You just happen to have a hair tie on you?"

I shrug, taking a pull of lemonade from one of the bottles I brought. "I keep one with me just in case."

It was on our second motorcycle ride on an ungodly windy day. She was good with the helmet on, but when we got to the shoreline, her hair whipped around her like a tornado, and she didn't have anything to secure it into a ponytail or one of those messy bun things women do. It's easy enough to put a band in my pocket when I grab my keys, wallet, and phone each day. Even when we were apart, if I left the house, I took a hair tie. It reminds me of her every time I reach in my pocket. And on days like today, I have one ready and waiting for her.

It's the small things…

"Just in case I need it?"

I grunt my response, watching her eyes soften and her breathing pick up. Fuck if my cock doesn't stir at the adoration on her lovely face. She loves me taking care of her. I'll do everything I can to keep that up for the rest of our lives.

She lays down her sandwich, holds up her dress and crawls to me. Stopping at my side, she gathers her hair and affixes it atop her head in a bun with the band I gave her.

My own sandwich forgotten, I push everything to the edge

of the blanket and cover the remaining food before commanding, "Lie down, Flower."

My heart picks up when she does as instructed.

Love her compliant, love her feisty, love her any way I can get her.

Good girl, I silently whisper for my own satisfaction.

Lying beside her, resting on my elbow, I run my hand up her leg till I reach the hem of her dress, letting it ride up as I caress upward to her hips. I squeeze, releasing her dress, and continue up, resting my hand on her ribs, her eyes locked on mine.

"I want to love you here on the site of our future home." I kiss the center of her chest. "You okay with that?"

She runs her fingers into my hair, scratching my scalp, making me want to purr and sink inside her as she does it again. "Yes, please."

I slide the straps of her sundress off her shoulders, tugging the fabric till her breasts are exposed. I suspected she wasn't wearing a bra, my naughty girl. I cup her head with the arm supporting my weight and lean in for a kiss. She meets me halfway, wrapping her arms around my shoulders and opening her sweet mouth, getting a lick in across my top lip before I'm on her, teasing her tongue with mine, intertwined and dancing, dancing, dancing.

Gripping her breast, I squeeze and tease her hard peaks one at a time, drawing out moan after moan. When she's pushing her tits into my hand, I break our kiss, moving down her jaw to her neck, taking a moment to savor the softness of her skin and suck over the pulse point in her neck. Finally making it to my destination, I suck in a taut nipple and relish her gasp and following moan.

"Reid." She fists my hair, holding me in place, urging me to continue.

Continue I do, but I add my hand to the mix, running it up her skirt, growling when I find her bare. "Where are your panties, Wildflower?"

"Oh, did I forget them?"

"Tease." I bite her nipple, running my fingers down her slit and back, spreading her moisture to her clit. She moans, spreading her legs, sucking in air when a breeze washes over us. "You like that? Your pussy on full display?"

"For you, yes," she gasps.

I tear myself from her breast long enough to watch as I slip my fingers inside her, pumping in and out. "Fuck, Daisy. I want in here. I always want inside you." The truth of that hits me hard, and how close I came to losing her.

She lifts her hips, fucking my fingers. "Please."

"Soon, baby. Soon." I need the feel of her breast in my mouth as I finger-fuck her, getting her there and making me stone-hard in dire need of plunging inside her.

I can't help grinding against her hip, alleviating the ache, the need to feel her wet pussy wrapped around my strained cock.

Pressing my palm against her mound, I stroke her insides, making her push and grind into my hand like wild woman. "Fucking hot, baby," I whisper across her lips.

"Need you," she whines.

"I got you." I've always got her.

I devour her mouth while she rides my hand, taking everything I'm giving in quick, needy thrusts of her hips, until she starts to shake and her movements become sloppy. Then I'm back on her nipples, sucking, licking, and biting.

In seconds, she shatters, calling my name, moaning and shaking, soaking my fingers as I continue to massage her G-spot till she's spent. The sound drives me crazy, amping up my need to sink in deep, bathing my cock in her wet heat.

"Holy…" my girls gasps as she falls limp on the blanket.

While she recovers, I undress, not missing her hungry gaze as she takes me in. "You like what you see?"

"I *love* what I see."

Damn, my girl. Hitting me in the right spot every time.

"I want you naked, Flower." I stroke my cock as she manages to sit up enough to wiggle her dress up over her head. "Good girl."

She flushes, making my cock bob like a tuning fork, looking for her and only her.

"On your hands and knees."

She slowly rolls over. Her ass hits the air first. I place a hand between her shoulder blades, keeping her head down. "You okay like this?"

"Yeah, I'm too weak to hold myself up anyway," she pants. The reason for her being short of breath is a lure to my cock, fuel to the fire burning deep inside me for my girl.

I settle in behind her, rubbing her ass cheeks, spreading

her for my viewing pleasure, making her moan and push back, begging to be filled. "If it's too much, you tell me."

"It's never too much."

I swat her ass. "If it is—"

"I'll tell you," she moans.

I swat the other cheek. She gifts me with another moan and a push back. I grip my cock, running the angry head through her wet folds, growling when she pushes back right as I'm at her opening, taking the tip inside her. I slam forward, holding her hips, and sink in all the way, cursing and praising her and sweet God in heaven.

The louder she screams and moans, the harder I thrust and growl my approval. "Taking me so good, Wildflower. Gonna come so fucking hard."

"Yes, yes, yes," she chants after every dirty suggestion and fantasy that falls from my mouth.

I've never been a talker, particularly during sex, but my girl draws it out of me: the dirty, the cherished, the awe-inspiring words and emotions all combine in a heated outpouring of love and naughty, naughty thoughts. Only for her.

Fuck. Not going to last.

"You need to come," I bark.

"I—" she screams and nearly collapses as she comes around my cock, only my grip on her hips keeping her steady I pour the last of my seed inside her, bellowing her name.

After a few more pumps and her breathing evens out, I collapse beside her, pulling her into my arms. "Love you." It's a groused endearment that in no way encapsulates the entirety of what I feel for her. The depth, the width, the enormity of my love can't accurately be represented by those two words.

She throws her leg over me, inching closer, giving me ideas. "Love you too."

When she's asleep a few moments later, I use her discarded dress to cover her ass in case anyone does decide to venture up here.

CHAPTER 25

REACHING FOR THE BACK OF HER NECK, I kiss her worried brow. "I'll be back in twenty-four hours. Don't worry. You need me, call. If I can't answer right away, know I'll call you back. You need something, call Mom and Dad. The number's on the fridge."

She pushes at my chest, rolling her eyes. "I have their numbers."

I pull her to me, wrapping my arms around her lush curves. This is harder than I thought. "Turner is off, so you can call him too."

"I'll be fine." She nuzzles into my neck. "Promise me you'll be safe."

Her hair fisted in my hand, I plant what I hope is a confident kiss to her sweet temptation of a mouth. "I will be. I'll see you around this time tomorrow. Maybe you could take off, spend the day with me?"

"I have a feeling your mom will be okay with that."

"Love you, Wildflower."

"Love you," her voice cracks, and it breaks something deep inside me.

I kiss her hair and promise, "This is my last season. I swear. I don't want to be apart from you any more than you do."

She nods and backs away, sniffing and wiping her eyes. "You'll be late."

Yeah, I probably already am. "See ya soon."

"Yep, see ya tomorrow."

I consider asking her to come spend the night in the hammock with me, but probably not the best idea since it'll be my first night back on the schedule and need rest, not a sexy distraction. I already passed medical and jumped through all of the red-tape hoopla. I'm physically ready to go.

It's my mental state in leaving her that's giving me doubts. My heart isn't in the job anymore—leaving her is even worse.

"Love you." I pause at the door.

She smiles and pushes. "Go. I'm fine. I survived years before I knew you, totally without you. I can survive one night without you."

I hate that. "Way to make a man feel needed." I kiss her hand before stepping back and taking the stairs two at a time.

"I love you too," she hollers before I close my truck door.

There it is.

I watch her as long as I can as I reverse and then turn, heading to town.

That was harder and yet easier than I anticipated. *She* made it easier by keeping her shit together. If she had broken down, I would have called and resigned right then.

But my Wildflower is strong and resilient. She can't be stamped out by a mere fire in her store and apartment that took everything that meant anything to her—except me. I survived. And now I will survive this season so we can get married and start living the rest of our lives together in a place we build from scratch that's perfect from the start.

I've just got to make it through the next twenty-four hours— keeping my commitments to my firehouse and my girl.

"How bad was it?" Mary rushes to me as soon as I enter the back of the Flower Mart.

"About what I expected. I didn't cry. Barely."

With a quick hug, she promises, "Well, it will get easier."

Will it? Do I want it to? The last thing I want is to become blasé about Reid's safety, about the possibility of him not coming home. Fear ripples through my body. I shake it off. I can't give in to it.

"The wildfires north of Redding are getting out of hand. His firehouse will more than likely be called in." She squeezes my hand. "It's the life of a firefighter's wife."

I know she means well. Warning me. Wanting me to be prepared. But I'm not sure how you prepare to send your significant other into harm's way. I'm not his wife yet, but even if I was, I wouldn't feel any differently about him having such a dangerous job. But resigning or not is up to him.

"Isn't your other son, the smoke jumper, based in Redding?" I try to steer the conversation off Reid.

"Yes. Gregary is just a year older than Reid at twenty-five. I worry about him. I wish he'd give up that dangerous life. Come home and work with his brothers."

"As a fireman?" I clarify as I'm not sure how much safer it is fighting fires in the city than in the forest.

"Yes." She smiles. "I know, Daisy, it doesn't seem much better, but believe me. It is."

What does that mean when Reid, Galant, and Turner are deployed to fight the wildfires? They'll all be in more danger, no doubt.

I spend the rest of the day doing everything and anything to keep my mind off Reid and fires—here or in Redding or wherever they are. The life of a firefighter is more than just fighting fires, but since that's my most recent experience, it's hard to think of much else. I lose count of how many silent prayers I say to bring him home safe to me every time he's away. His brothers too.

Once I'm home, the house is too quiet. I put on the TV for background noise and jump in the shower. When I come out, there's a knock at the door.

"Turner?"

He smiles, holding up boxes of pizza and a six-pack of beer. "I thought you could use some company."

I could cry in thanks, but for his sake, I hold it in. "You're amazing."

"That's what the ladies tell me," he teases as he enters, heading for the kitchen. "How many slices you want?"

"Is all of it too much?"

Chuckling, he places the pizzas on the coffee table. "I'll just leave these here and grab some plates."

"I can get—"

"Nope—" He holds out his hand. "You find us something to watch, preferably a mindless action movie."

"I can do that." I plop down on the couch, checking the guide. Definitely something that doesn't involve fire.

"*Pluto Nash* is what you picked?!" Turner shakes his head, handing me a beer and a water. "I didn't know what you'd want to drink."

"Both. It's Eddie Murphy. How bad can it be?"

"Bad. It can be really bad." He motions toward the remote. "Go ahead. I get to pick the next one, and you can't complain."

"Deal."

I consume more pizza than I've ever eaten, thankful he brought two so I don't feel bad about eating so much.

"Is pepperoni your fave, then?" He watches as I take another bite.

"*Pizza* is my favorite, but, yeah, I like pepperoni, sausage, hamburger, and supreme."

"But if you had to pick one?"

"Pepperoni."

"I knew I liked you." He high-fives me.

He's a dork but easy to be around. I like Galant too, but he's more intense. I feel like I need to have a serious conversation when he's around. I'd never choose *Pluto Nash* as the movie of choice if he were here instead. He seems more like a *The Shawshank Redemption* kinda guy.

"You doing okay?"

I still, catching the concern in his voice. "Yeah. I miss him, but he'll be home in the morning."

"There's nothing that would stop Reid from coming home to you." He's so certain.

I can think of a few terrifying things that could keep us apart, but instead, I pray he's right.

I open the door to find Turner in the kitchen making breakfast, pizza boxes on the coffee table, and a pillow and blanket folded up on the couch. It's not a surprise to see him as his Charger is parked outside. But it does fill my heart with peace knowing he was watching over my girl. I didn't even have to ask.

"You hungry?" He slides a cup of coffee my direction.

"Starved. Where's—"

"Shower."

I leave the coffee and start down the hall—

"No *Bow Chicka Bow Wow*. Breakfast is almost ready."

"Roger."

I halt just inside our bedroom when I find Daisy slipping on her panties. I quietly close the door. "Morning, Flower."

She whips around, her eyes wide. "I'd hoped to be dressed before you got here."

"I'd hoped you'd be naked in bed waiting for me." I kiss her neck up to her ear and whisper, "Missed you."

She sighs into our embrace, worry leaving her one breath at a time. "Missed you too." She rises to her tippy toes and kisses me softly and tenderly. "I can't imagine you'd want me naked in bed with your brother here."

"Not unless I was here too. So, if you want…" I squeeze her ass. "You can get in bed, and I'll kick him out."

"We can't do that. He's cooking and brought me dinner last night and stayed to be sure I was really okay. But later—"

"I'm fucking you till you're screaming my name."

She pats my chest then backs up, grabbing another tempting sundress off the bed. "So, like normal then?" She flashes me a devious smile.

"Yeah, Flower. Like every damn time I love on you."

Her blush is perfect and only makes me more determined to eat and usher our guest out.

I kiss her bare shoulder. "Soon, baby. Soon."

CHAPTER 26

THE NEWS CAME SHORTLY AFTER HE'D returned from his first shift at his firehouse. The wildfires just past Redding are spreading. Other firehouses in California were called in too. Reid's Round Rock Fire Station is to send as many as they can spare in two days' time.

That was two days ago.

I watch him pack, trying to hide my worry and nervousness over him leaving.

"I'll call you every day," he promises. "I'll try to make it at night or first thing in the morning, but it'll just depend on where I am and the reception, and the shifts are kind of wild. Turner is staying. He'll get official word and let you know when I'm unreachable. It's not uncommon to lose communication for a few days. So don't panic if that happens."

"H-how many times have you done this?" This time, I can't stop the tears as they fall.

"This will be my fourth year. Gregary will be there too… somewhere." He glances up, spotting my crumbling state. "Flower."

"I know." I swipe at my face and try to laugh. "I can't help it. Besides missing the heck out of you, I'm scared. What if—"

"Don't." He wraps me in his warm embrace. "I'm coming back. This is not where we end."

I'm having déjà vu all over again from the night of the fire at my place. "Just stay safe. Make good choices. Keep Galant alive and Gregary, if you even see him."

"Oh, I'll see him. He'll make a point of dropping in on us to save the day or something heroic." He kisses my head. "I know you'll worry, but don't make yourself sick over it. Promise you'll eat, sleep, keep busy."

"I've no doubt your mom will be sure I do."

He chuckles. "Let Turner stay as much as he wants and you can stand. He'll be busy taking up the slack at the firehouse, but he'll come check on you and give you news as he hears it. He's also bringing the bedroom furniture we ordered for the guest room to set it up. He might bring a few guys to help."

"He doesn't have—"

"He wants to. You're family. We take care of our own. Mom may try to convince you to stay with them, but don't feel pressure to say *yes*."

He cups my face in his massive hands. "Promise me you won't sit here alone and fret. I don't want you getting—"

"If I get depressed like I did while we were apart, I'll reach out to your mom, Turner, or even Sage," I promise. I've no intention of going down that road again.

"You could go stay with your dad if that would make it easier."

My Sequoia not leaving would make it easier.

"No, I want to be here in our house. Besides, they're breaking ground on our house in two weeks. I want to be here. Your dad will have it under control, but I'd like to watch, keep up with their progress."

"He knows not to make any design changes without your approval. So do the architect and foreman." He kisses my brow. "I'm hoping I won't be gone longer than a few weeks."

We didn't talk specifics. I thought it would be like a week, two tops.

He holds my head to his chest. "I'm going to miss the fuck out of you, Daisy. Promise you'll take care of yourself."

"I promise. You too."

"Promise, baby." He pats my ass. "Let me finish packing, then I'll say a proper goodbye."

A proper goodbye? I have no idea what one of those looks like…

I find out fifteen minutes later where he has me pinned to the wall, fingering me until I come, until Galant nearly busts his horn honking.

"You're so hot when you come." Reid sucks on my neck, leaving a new mark in his spot. "I'll miss every inch of you."

176

Panting, I kiss him for dear life, fueling it with all my love and safe prayers. "I love you, Reid. You better bring your sexy ass home to me."

"Wildflower, nothing can keep me from you, especially not a little fire."

"I'm holding you to that."

"Good." He kisses my nose. "Love you. Talk soon."

And just like that, he's gone with the smell of me on his hand, a smile on his face, and a stiffy in his pants that has to be uncomfortable.

"Took you fucking long enough. We're late," Galant barks as I climb in his Suburban.

"They won't leave without us." I adjust my pants, wishing I'd taken the time to fuck my girl properly this morning. Though I loved on her most of the night, one more time wouldn't have hurt. If I were trying to get her pregnant, last night would have been the night.

But we're not. Not yet.

We want more time together first.

"You sure you have everything?" I glanced at the bed of his truck when I set my pack in there, but I didn't take inventory.

"Affirmative."

"Are we picking up anyone else?"

"No, Damon and Judge are already on their way. We'll meet up in Redding."

"In Redding?" I thought we'd go farther than that. Though I guess no one wants to abandon their cars close to the fire zone.

"Yeah. We'll get transportation from there with the local CCC." He glances at me and down to my left leg. "You sure you're ready for this? You've been off for nearly four months."

"I'm in the best shape of my life. I've worked out every day as soon as I was released to do so. I can hike and climb. I have a brace for stability if it gets bad. I'm good," I assure him. I probably could have bowed out with having just returned to active duty. Turner would have gladly taken my place. But it was *my* name called. It's *my* duty to serve. And if anything happened to Turner in my place, I'd never forgive myself.

"You stick with me."

Not this again. "We go where we're told. You know they won't keep us together."

"We did that one year."

"Yeah, because you bullied the guy into making me come with your battalion because it was my first year. This isn't my first year. You need to focus on the fire and staying alive, not worrying about me." Though I do appreciate his big brother worry. "I got this. But you should know: this is my last season. I'm hanging it up after this."

He sighs. "I had a feeling. Dad will be happy."

"He hung in till retirement," I remind him.

"It's a different time. He's thinking grandbabies. Now that he's on the other side, watching us put our lives on the line, he's changed his tune. He thinks we should give five years and get out.

It's enough sacrifice. Especially after the fire at Daisy's. He didn't take a breath until he knew you two were going to be okay."

"What about you?"

He shrugs. "I don't know. I'll stick with it until something better comes along."

"You need to find a woman. She'll put things in perspective."

"Like you?"

"Exactly. But I never loved firefighting like you and Turner, and definitely not like Gregary."

He laughs. "No one loves it like Gregary."

"Truth. Hey, have you talked to Theo? She's not returning my calls. I haven't seen her since we've been back."

"She's going through some stuff. She's okay though." He doesn't seem too sure.

"Anything you can share?"

"Not my story, man."

That's always been our way. We don't tattle on each other, and we don't share details that aren't ours to tell. But if you need something, say the word, and we're there. No questions asked.

It's a long drive to Redding. My body is stiff, and I'm ready for a nap by the time we get there. When we pull into the fire station where we'll leave our truck and meet up with Damon and Judge, I text Daisy.

Me: *We made it to Redding.*

Wildflower: *Be safe. Miss you already.*

Me: *Miss you too. Love you.*

Wildflower: *Love you too.*

CHAPTER 27

THE FIRST FEW DAYS PASS IN A BLUR. JUDGE and I are with one of the Redding California Conservative Corps (CCC) crews. Galant and Damon have each been placed with separate crews. I see or hear from Galant on a daily basis, but we're rarely in the same place at the same time.

We've primarily been working on fire breaks to slow or hopefully stop the fires from spreading, by clearing logs and brush, basically eliminating the fire's fuel. But fire is a beautiful, deadly, determined beast. If there's a way, she'll find it. We hike four to six miles a day, sometimes coming back to the main camp or a different one. All my gear goes with me, as I don't know when or if I'll return to base camp. It's likely to move when the fire moves.

When I get downtime, Daisy is first on my list to call, then I call Turner most times as well. My parents and brothers are in a group chat and how I let them know I'm okay. I'd include Daisy, but I'm worried someone will say something, give too much info we're used to as a family that might terrify her. She doesn't know this life. She hasn't grown up with it. I'd rather communicate with her directly anyway, keeping the details pertinent and not inflammatory.

I'm exhausted, but before I eat or attempt to clean up, I call my girl.

"Reid." She answers on the first ring like she was sitting around waiting on me.

"Hey, Flower. My phone is low on battery, so I only have a few minutes. I don't know if I'll be able to charge it. My back-up battery is already drained, and my solar charger is dead."

"So I might not hear from you?"

"Not unless I can get it charged. You okay? Anything I should know?"

"I'm good. I love you and miss you. Don't worry. Stay safe," she quickly rambles.

"Love you. Miss you. I think it'll be four or five more days." Thirty-three days is the average to put a wildfire out, and this one has been going for twenty-seven.

"Just come home."

I know she means safe and sound at the end. "Wild horses can't keep me away."

"You have a thing for *wild* things." She laughs and sniffs.

"Only my *wild* girl. Don't cry, Flower. I'll see you soon. I gotta go. Love you."

"Love you—"

The line drops, my phone dead, cutting her off.

She's fine. She's emotional, which is to be expected. But she's fine. She's safe.

I look at our makeshift camp. There are no chargers here. There's no backup generator. We're sleeping out in the open tonight. Too late to get back to the closest camp, most of us too exhausted to even consider the trek. I dig in my pack for food and settle in for a long night with thoughts of my Flower keeping me company.

The front door flying open startles me until I see Turner trying to balance one end of a box spring while keeping the door from hitting the wall.

"Shit, sorry." He quickly grabs the mattress.

"I didn't know you were coming this early. Thank God I'm dressed." I rush to hold the door out of his way.

He smirks, giving me the once-over. "Me and the guys wouldn't mind."

Eew. "Yeah, tell your brother that."

He blanches. "On second thought, I'll call first next time." His voice trails down the hall to the guest bedroom.

I smile at the guys who follow, carrying the other half of the king box spring mattress. *I should make more coffee.*

Turner comes back down the hall. The rest of the guys head out the door as he stops in the kitchen. "You okay?"

"Yeah—" I point at the coffeemaker. "You want me to make more coffee?"

"That'd be great." He notices my Flower Mart t-shirt. "You working today?"

"Yes. I was just getting ready to head out." Now I feel like I should stay.

"If you don't mind starting the coffee, I brought stuff to make them breakfast. Do you mind if I still do that here?"

"Make yourself at home."

"Are the sheets and stuff you want on the bed in the guest room?"

"Everything is in that bag on the floor. I washed the sheets and put them back in it."

"Then, you leave, and I'll get this settled."

"You sure?"

"Yeah, are you okay if I stay here tonight? I can make dinner so it's ready when you get home."

Seriously? "I'm not going to pass up dinner and company."

He laughs, heading for the door. "Okay, do what you need to do, and I'll see you later."

"Turner," I stop him at the threshold, "thanks for... everything. It means a lot to have you around."

He winks on a nod. "Anything for Reid's girl."

I blush at the reminder. Proud and giddy, I start their coffee, grab my tumbler with my coffee already in it, my purse and head for the door, saying goodbye as I pass the guys bringing in another load.

It doesn't take long to get to the Flower Mart. Though I do miss making up bouquets on the regular, I don't miss having deadlines and deliveries. Once I arrive, I pretty much handle what Mary would do with helping customers, allowing her to spend more time in the office on paperwork and the admin tasks she usually had to do after hours, thus shortening her day.

There are other employees for the heavy lifting and running the registers. I mainly flit around seeing if anyone needs help, ensuring the overflow in back gets moved to the front to restock what's sold. As for deliveries, they're usually early morning before I get here, so Mary or one of her floor managers handles that. I'm still finding my place, trying to be useful and earn my keep.

She was even kind enough to bring on Stacy from my store. That was a nice surprise but maybe a little weird since I'm no longer her boss. Will I be again? Not yet, anyway.

Mary keeps talking about making me a co-owner. I'm not ready for that. I need to be sure this is what I want and see what Reid ends up doing. If he works the farm, I might rather do that with him than be here. She doesn't grow enough to cover all the flowers Flower Mart offers, but she does provide a large portion of her product herself, instead of buying from a wholesaler or directly from other growers in the area.

I set my purse in the office before meeting her out front. "Morning, Mary."

She side-hugs me. "Good morning. Galant called this morning. He said he saw Reid yesterday, and he was good. Galant thinks they may have another five days or so."

"That's what Reid said when I talked to him yesterday. His phone died. I don't know when we'll hear from him next."

"Galant said he was having trouble finding a place to charge his phone too. I'm not sure why they don't have solar chargers." Or magical forcefields that protect and help real life heroes.

"Reid has a solar charger, but he said it's out of charge too. Maybe they're not in one place long enough to charge it during the day." Does the fire's smoke coat the atmosphere, making it difficult for sunlight to reach their camp at a level that allows solar to be effective?

"We may have to rely on the updates from the firehouse. Turner will let us know when he hears something."

I love Mary, but she likes to talk about the wildfires in detail. And if I'm going to survive Reid's absence, I need something to do that's *not* fixating on his safety. I look around the bustling crowd. "What can I do?"

"I thought I might show you how to do the ordering when things die down."

"Sounds good. I'm going to see if anyone needs help."

"See you in a bit."

I head off to numb my mind and have a break from worry.

CHAPTER 28

I T'S ON THE SEVENTH DAY THAT I PASS GALANT as his team is heading down the trail—probably done for the day—and we're heading up to clear more brush and trees, hopefully stopping the fire's progress—this direction anyway.

Staying in formation, we turn, walking backwards.

"You okay?"

"Yeah, you?" he hollers.

"Yeah. Phone's dead. Call Daisy if you can," I holler back as the distance pulls him farther way.

"Affirmative. Stay tight." With a wave of his hand, he turns, looking back up the hill and then to me. He's worried.

But he always worries. I try not to let it set off any warning bells. Yet it is late to be heading to a new location. We were on another ridge and diverted when the wind changed directions.

"That your brother?" Ricky, one of the guys in the CCC crew I've gotten to know, asks from behind.

"Yeah. I haven't seen him in four days." Though we've texted in that time just to let the other know we're okay.

"Man, I can't imagine having my brother here."

"I've got another one here as well. He's a smoke jumper. I haven't seen him yet. Then another brother at home holding down the fort. He's a firefighter too."

"Four brothers? All firefighters?"

"Yep."

"Man, my mom would die if all her kids did what I do."

"My dad and grandfather were firemen too. My mom is used to it."

"That's quite a legacy."

"Yeah." I guess it is.

Do I want that for my kids?

Seeing it from Ricky's perspective makes it seem cooler than it is. He's not considering one call could take out me and my two brothers. Being in the same firehouse probably isn't smart for that reason alone. But Galant likes watching over us, and I like working with my brothers. Honestly, it's probably the main reason I became a firefighter in the first place. Yes, legacy, but primarily, I wanted to hang with my brothers, be a part of their world.

Am I really ready to give this up? The job is more than fighting fires. We're a unit, a family, relying on each other on the job and off.

Half a mile more, we reach our destination. The sun is still high in the sky. I wipe my brow, dig in with my Pulaski and get to clearing a path. The guys in my crew are right alongside me.

It feels like hours when I take a water break, but in reality it's only been thirty minutes. As soon as I put my thermos away, the hairs on the back of my neck stand on end as the wind picks up.

I'm not the only one who notices. Our supervisor is talking on the walkie as we survey our surroundings.

"It's the witching hour." Judge comes up next to me.

I grunt my acknowledgment, taking in the increased winds, not much humidity, and the sun still high as fuck in the sky. Not good.

In the distance, the crackling of the fire sounds closer than it did before.

"Pack it up. The fire's turning," our crew's supervisor calls from the end of the line.

I put away my tools and throw on my pack. In a matter of a minute, we're double-timing it back the way we came.

The knock at the door has me jumping to answer it. I haven't heard from Reid today. Galant called hours ago advising he'd seen Reid on the trail and asked that he call me.

It was a short call. Just long enough to confirm Galant was okay. They hadn't seen Gregary yet, but by all accounts, he's fine. And then, of course, the part about him seeing and talking to Reid.

I want to talk to him. It's been two days since I've heard his voice. He sent me a quick text the day before yesterday, but he never replied to mine. I'm assuming his phone is dead again, or he doesn't have reception.

Before I get to the door, Turner opens it.

"Hey." I step back, giving him room to enter. His eyes are a little wild. "Everything okay?"

He fidgets with his keys before pocketing them. "We just got word."

"No." I back up till I hit the couch.

Turner reaches for me, gripping my hand. "He's not... His crew was working the line. The wind picked up. The fire changed direction. The last they heard from them was that they there were trapped."

I crumble.

Turner catches me. "Don't lose hope, Daisy. They have fire shelters that keep them safe—minimize burns—even in the heart of the fire."

"You mean they're going to *burn*?" I can't even... Oh my god!

"I *mean*, they're stuck. Fire is unpredictable. It can change direction in a blink of an eye. But if they prepare, get under their fire shelters, there's a high probability he'll be fine."

"You don't seem too sure." I manage to stand on my own, long enough to sit on the couch.

He swipes his hand over his face. "He's my brother, Daisy. I know what can happen. So, yeah, I'm worried. But I'm not giving up hope. And neither should you."

"I'm not giving up." I'll never give up on my Sequoia.

Filled with determination instead of sadness, I go to our

bedroom, grab a bag and start stuffing clothes in it. "Tell your mom I'll be back, but I don't know when."

"What?" Turner fills the doorway. "What are you doing?"

"I'm going to Redding."

"No! You can't." He steps forward, grabbing my arm, halting my progress. "Daisy, he wouldn't… What are you going to do?"

I wrench free. He doesn't grab for me again as I continue to pack. "I'm going to be there for when he needs me."

"Fuck." He runs his hand through his hair. "I'm coming with you. Reid wouldn't want you going alone."

"You'd better pack, then."

"I already am."

I cock a brow. "Really?"

"I have the bag I brought to stay here. It has everything I need."

"What about work?"

"I'm off for the next two days."

"Okay. Call your parents. Let them know. I hope your mom won't fire me. But I'm going, either way."

CHAPTER 29

WE'VE DIVERTED THREE TIMES, TRYING TO escape the path of the fire. Wind direction keeps changing, which means the fire has circled around us. We've searched for any means of escape. There is none.

With adrenaline pumping through our veins like oxygen, our crew of twenty starts to deploy, digging in, clearing out debris—any fuel that can feed the fire. We want the fire to pass by without burning on top of us when we get in our fire shelters. The farther we can keep it from our shelters, the better. Thankfully, we're at the bottom of a ridge of boulders with little vegetation below. We work to remove all vegetation to expose as much soil as possible.

My heart is pounding like a jackhammer. We have maybe

ten minutes before we need to take shelter and pray we've done all we can to not only survive but survive with minimal injuries.

Mary couldn't have been more supportive when she heard we were driving to Redding. She made Turner and me promise we wouldn't drive farther toward the fires. I had no problem making that promise. Turner, on the other hand—

"Turner Warren Ashford, you promise me right now. I've got three sons in that fire. Don't make me worry over you too. I can't take it."

Begrudgingly he agrees, "I promise I won't volunteer, Mom. What if they ask me to go?"

Not missing a beat, she replies, "Your firehouse is relying on you. They sent four men, two of them my sons. You have two days before you have to be back here to work. This town and your crew depend on you. Don't let us down."

That was a few hours ago. We're fifty miles outside of Redding. We've been lost in our own thoughts. I'm afraid to ask questions I'm not sure I want the answers to. My thoughts are consumed with prayers and begging for Reid to be alright—unharmed.

The last of the miles slip by like molasses. The music is low, barely audible over the sound of the highway as Turner pushes the boundaries of the legal speed limit. I only had to remind him one time that getting a ticket will only slow us down. Not that I didn't want him to race the entire way there, burning out his engine in the process.

As we reach the city limits, his phone rings. We share a glance as he grips my hand and answers.

The heat pushes down on us as the roar of the fire closes in. Our tools and gear discarded, we take cover in our fire shelters, holding the edges down with our feet and arms, face down in the dirt, praying for mercy.

I've done this in training, but I've never actually had to do it in the four years I've been fighting wildfires. Neither have any of my brothers, including Gregary, who is the most likely to have experienced it before, given his dangerous job of jumping into the front of the fire, trying to stop it, avert it, delay it. Anything to slow its progress.

I can imagine how strange it looks to see rows and rows of shiny silver man-sized burritos as we take cover under our individual shelters—twenty of them. I'm closest to the ridge of rocks; only the most experienced of the wildlands firefighters are positioned on the outer edges.

Under the crackle of the fire moving ever closer, I can make out the low murmurs of my crew praying, comforting others, and finally the reminder to conserve oxygen. The deadly gases that could kill us are blocked out by the shelters if we've secured them well enough, but that means whatever air is in here with us is it. Before it gets too late, I lift my right hand just a fraction to let in fresh air, but it's only a second before smoke seeps in too. I slam down my hand, closing my eyes, picturing my Flower, and silently pray, fighting the panic and natural inclination to run.

"It's Dad," Turner says to me seconds before he answers. "Dad?"

"Is Daisy with you?" Roman's voice comes through the car speakers.

"Yes. We're just pulling into Redding."

"You made good time—"

"You have news?" Turner cuts off his father, his grip on my hand tightening, maybe as much for him as for me.

"I just spoke to your chief. They've made contact with Reid's crew. They've deployed—"

"Shit." Turner shoots a concerned look at me before focusing on the road.

"—an Airtanker is heading their way."

"W-what does that mean?"

"It'll drop water or fire retardant on them to put out the fire and make a path for them to escape," their dad explains. "Also, I've booked you two hotel rooms. I'll text you the details."

"Thanks, Dad. I'll let you know when I have any news."

"Same." Roman is quiet for a moment. "Daisy, I know you're worried. But don't be. This is great news. We'll know more shortly. Hang in there."

I nod, the lump in my throat keeping me from replying.

Turner gives me a knowing smile and squeezes my hand. "She's good, Dad. I got her until Reid does."

194

My tears start to fall at the truth of his statement. "You're a good brother," I manage to whisper despite my trembling chin.

Turner squeezes my hand, letting me know he heard me as his father continues, "Your mother's pacing. So call—"

"I will. Talk soon. Love you."

"Love you both."

The line disconnects. I slump into my seat. Mind racing.

Turner taps my hand. "Questions?"

"What does *deployed* mean?" I only understand it in a vague military context.

"It means they couldn't escape, so they had to take cover under their fire shelters."

I nod as if I fully understand what that means. At least they know where they are? I swipe at my tears, taking a breath, trying to think happy thoughts. "Can we get a drink?"

He laughs. "Like alcohol?"

"No. Like a Coke."

"Yeah, let's pick up food before we check in at the hotel." He squeezes my hand before releasing it. "He's going to be okay, Daisy. I feel it."

Thank God one of us does. Though, deep down I feel like I'd know if he was—

I can't even think it.

The sound of trees bursting as they're consumed by fire and the whirl of the flames and wind roars all around us. The heat is bearable, but the fire shelters can only take so much before they start to melt.

I swear I hear the squawk of a radio. I tip my head, listening.

Nothing but the sounds and smells of devastation fill my senses.

Then I hear it.

The rumble of the radio again and a shout. But I can't make it out.

Endless seconds pass. The heat increases; my body is stiff from holding still, ensuring the shelter is sealed all around me, but my job is to stay still and wait, trusting the other crews to do their job.

A loud roar passes over us. It almost sounds like an air—

Splash

I'm hit with something cool and wet. My fire shelter hisses, and the temperature drops considerably.

Then there's another roar passing overhead, and this time, I know it's an airplane. I clench, ready for the water to drop again.

But it never comes.

Instead, I hear radio chatter and "All clear!" in the distance that is repeated down the line and all around me.

Is it true?

I slowly peek out just as I hear, "Reid! Is there a Reid Ashford here?!"

I know that voice.

Without a second thought, I climb to my feet, letting my fire shelter slide off my back. "Gregory?!"

CHAPTER 30

I T'S BEEN HOURS WAITING FOR TURNER TO GET back from the fire station. He left shortly after we checked in and ate the food we picked up. I've showered, texted with Sage and my dad, but my phone has been silent ever since. I don't want to bug Turner, as I know he'll call or text as soon as he has an update.

I'm about ready to order room service just to give myself something to do besides stare at my phone and flip through channel after channel on the TV. I even tried watching the news, but the fires have been going on for so long, their coverage is in short blips, and I have no idea where Reid is to even attempt to correlate their updates into something—anything—that would apply to him. It's nerve-racking to watch and hope, praying for any morsel of news that would bring good news for Reid, for all of them.

A swift knock on my door brings me to my feet seconds before the adjoining room's door unlocks and I hear the whoosh of it opening. My feet are stuck to the carpet, waiting, preparing to hear what Turner has to say.

Through the open doorway that joins our rooms, Turner walks in. His eyes are red-rimmed, and his cheeks are flushed.

My knees nearly give out as the blood drains from my head, making me dizzy.

"Fuck." He rushes me, gripping my shoulders. "No, Daisy, it's—"

Knock. Knock. This time the person on the other side is more demanding.

I glance at Turner and then the door. Normally he'd be the one to answer it.

He whispers, "I think that's for you."

It can't be.

On wobbly legs, I make it to the door and open it just as Reid lifts his hand—

"OhmyholyGrandmaJean!" I screech, tackling him, making him take a step back until he steadies us.

"Wildflower." He picks me up, burying his head in my neck. "Fuck, you smell good."

"Reid." I'm full-on bawling as he carries me inside the room, letting the door shut behind us.

"I got you." He moves to cup the back of my head. "Wild horses, baby."

I cry harder.

Shuffling in the room reminds me we're not alone. "We'll give you some privacy," Turner offers.

"Give us a bit. Thanks." Reid sits on the bed as the adjoining door clicks closed. "Let me see you," he urges.

I slowly relinquish my death grip on his neck, wiping my face with my sleeves. "I'm a mess."

"You're perfect." His brown eyes caress my face as he tenderly runs his thumbs under my eyes and over my cheeks. "My beautiful Wildflower."

More tears. "I don't think they'll ever stop."

He kisses my wet cheeks before running his lips over mine. "They will. You need time. I may shed a few tears before the night's out."

"Are you really alright?" My voice trembles in time with my chin.

"I am. I promise. And I'm done. No more fires for me." His soulful eyes seem older than when I saw him last.

"You resigned?"

"I handed in my resignation *before* I left. No matter how this wildfire went, I knew I couldn't put our future in jeopardy again. I'm done, baby."

"Your family—"

"Talked to them. Gregary actually helped rescue us."

"And Galant?"

"He's still there, but he's coming home in a few days. Two brother in that fire is enough. Plus, they think they're close to extinguishing it." He kisses my neck. "It'll all be over soon."

I take a stuttered breath. "I think I've aged a hundred years. I thought—"

"I know, and I'm sorry about that." A kiss to the other cheek. "It's done. At least for us."

"I want to be happy, but I don't want you to feel like you've giving up too much. I don't want you to resent me in a few years."

"Never." A kiss to my nose. "The only regret I'd ever have is missing out on a future with you."

This man. "I love you. Thank you for coming home to me."

His smile is tender as he presses his lips to mine. "Always coming home to you, because wherever you are *is* home."

"Reid."

"Baby." Another kiss. "Let me love on you."

"Please. Make me forget I almost lost you."

Our collective sigh is swallowed in our kiss as he slowly, tenderly undresses me with unhurried movements and loving caresses.

There's no rush, no timetable, no expiration date.

Tears well up when I see the state of my Sequoia's body marred by bruises, cuts, and small burns. He cups my cheek as he covers my body with his. "It'll all heal. Nothing's permanent other than my love for you."

Damn. How'd I get so lucky?

He settles between my legs, forcing mine wider with his knee as he rocks his hardness against my folds in an easy rhythm with our kiss.

There's no rush, no time table, no expiration date.

On a silent plea, he fills me, taking my breath and feeding me his groans as our tongues tangle and our hands explore.

Rocking. Rocking. Rocking.

He slips in and out of me, whispering words of praise and love between kisses, letting me catch my breath before he steals it again and again.

Over and over.

Cherished.

Savored.

Wanted.

Needed.

Each thrust of his hips punctuates the emotions swimming between us.

"Going to love you for the rest of our lives." He swivels his hips, stealing my moan and kissing his approval down my neck, sucking, sucking, sucking, until his mark is made and I'm coming undone.

For him.

Only ever for him.

Waves of tremors set off along my body when he growls his release, calling my name. Filling me. Filling me. Filling me.

"Love you forever," I whisper into his shoulder when he gifts me with the weight of his body, too exhausted to move.

"And ever and ever." He nuzzles into my neck, teasing and kissing his mark. Sliding sideways, half on me, half-off. "The next big adventure is marriage. You ready?"

"I can't wait."

"Good, 'cause I don't want to wait."

"I'll marry you anywhere, anytime. You name it."

"Ten days."

I laugh. "Why ten days?"

"That's how long I'm going to need to love on you before I can bear to let you out of my sight."

"Ten days is all you need?"

"You're right. It's not enough. I'll never want to be away from you. A million years will never be enough."

"It's a good thing we have eternity, then."

"Eternity." He kisses my shoulder. "Sounds about right."

THE END

Can't get enough? Want to know what's next for Reid and Daisy?
Keep reading for their **Epilogue** and a chance to get exclusive **BONUS SCENES** for newsletter subscribers.
https://dl.bookfunnel.com/98qjnc6pgy

Are you a fan of alphaholes and sports romances?
Meet the men of my *Black Ops MMA* Series. They're tough, determined, and sometimes too alpha for their own good. NO MERCY is Book 1 in the series. Gabriel "No Mercy" Stone fell hard for his best friend's woman. To hide his feelings, he ignored her and treated her like dirt. But when things go south with her boyfriend, Gabriel is there to pick up the pieces.
When it comes to protecting his Angel, he has no mercy.

Are best friend's sister, friends to lovers, and second chances more your style?
Then check out my Until You series. Book 1, *Until You Set Me Free*, is a heart-wrenching romance about a millionaire in the making and his best friend's younger sister. Joseph is everything Samantha is afraid to want, yet she's never wanted to be noticed so badly in her life. Samantha shouldn't even be on Joseph's radar, and yet she is from the day she walks in the room, making him want what's not his to take.
Some loves are just destined to be,
regardless of how hard you fight it.

This is a dream for me to be able to share my love of writing with you. If you liked this book, please consider leaving a review on Amazon and/or on Goodreads.

Personal recommendations to your friends and loved ones are a great compliment too.
Please share, follow, join my newsletter, and help spread the word—let everyone know how much you love Reid and Daisy.

EPILOGUE

A FEW HOURS LATER

QUIETLY, I DISENTANGLE FROM MY Wildflower, taking a moment to watch her sleep, sated and peaceful, the tracks of tears still fresh on her lovely face. A whispered "thank you" leaves my lips. *Thank you for getting me home to my girl.*

I pull on a t-shirt and boxer briefs and tap on Turner's adjoining door. It's not late, but they could be out. Firefighters respond differently when faced with their own mortality. I'm not sure if Judge would want to go out drinking or hang out in peaceful normality. Either way, Turner would be there to support him in whatever he needed.

It only takes a few seconds for his door to open, the sound of the TV coming through. Concern in his eyes turns to understanding as he backs up, opening his door all the way, allowing me to slip in before the noise wakes Daisy.

"You okay?" he asks before the door clicks shut behind me.

"I'm good." I spot their room service cart at the door. I'm glad they ate. Their room is identical to ours except it has two queen beds instead of our one king. "What are you guys watching?"

"*The Hangover.*" Judge laughs from his bed, taking a sip of beer, his eyes not leaving the screen. "Everything alright?" His tired eyes flick to me before returning to the movie.

"Yeah, all good. I wanted to check in. I was thinking we could head home tomorrow, not early. Sleep in, grab breakfast around ten-ish and then hit the road."

Turner scratches his chest on a yawn. "Sounds good. Just rap on the door when you wake up, and we'll get ready."

"Sure." I pause, contemplating my next words. "Thanks again for looking after Daisy, for bringing her here. You have no idea—" my voice cracks, flooded by remorse for what could have happened and thankfulness for what didn't.

Instantaneously, I'm in his strong embrace. "I'm glad you're okay. No need to thank me. I wanted to be here, and I'd never let her face all of this alone."

He's a good man. He may play a fool at times, but deep down, he's a standup guy.

Someday, if he ever decides to settle down, I'll do the same for him: look after his girl when he's not able to. Hopefully, it won't be a life-or-death type of situation. But in our—*his*—line of work, it's a strong possibility.

"Night," I offer as I return to my room.

Back on my side, I close and lock our door. I'm not taking any chances on them opening it to find us in a private moment.

"You're not tired?" Daisy turns, stretching, the swell of her breasts just peeking above the covers.

I pull off my shirt. "I just wanted to check on the guys." Dropping my boxer briefs, I climb on the bed, hovering over her. "I didn't mean to wake you."

She slides her hand up my chest, making my muscles tighten. When she runs her fingers through my hair, I fight the urge to purr as I lean into her touch. Her nails on my scalp send a shiver tingling down my spine with a direct hit to my cock. I focus on her green eyes that are thankfully tear-free as they glow in the moonlight shining in from a split in the curtains.

"You didn't wake me." Her brow furrows as she scans my face. "Is it hard to settle down after... an adrenaline rush?"

I kiss the curve of her neck before falling beside her. "Sometimes. A little." It's hard to settle the *what is* with the *what ifs*, and I'm racked with the *what ifs* at the moment.

She tugs at the covers, encouraging me to join her underneath. The sight of her naked, and the heat seeping into me from the warmth she trapped under the covers sends blood southward. I grip her waist, tugging her to me, covers be damned. "Love you so fucking much, Flower."

Today. Tomorrow. Always.

She kisses my right pec before granting me her eyes. "Love you, Reid. So damn much." The crack in her voice teeters in my heart. She knows what we could have lost today.

I roll toward her, wrapping her in my arms, relishing the warmth of her body pressing into mine as I run my hands along her silky skin. "I need to love you."

She presses her mouth to my neck, licking and sucking, making me groan as I harden between us. "I'd hoped you'd say that." Her breath teases my skin as she kisses across my jaw.

"Baby," I groan, falling to my back as she moves over me. "You never have to wait." I softly grip the side of her neck before sliding my hand into her hair. "Take what you need."

Her eyes close as she straddles my hips, slowly grinding against my needy cock. Her hands brace on my chest with her fingers gripping and kneading my pecs. Turning her head, she nuzzles my hand as I loosen my fist in her hair. Her skin is so fucking soft under my callused fingers. She runs her tongue along my thumb before opening her mouth.

"Oh fuck," I gasp as she closes her lips around my thumb and starts to suck. My hips buck with the need to drill home.

As she moves against me, my cock peeks in and out of her pussy lips. I release her hip to caress up her body to her breasts, plumped between her arms still braced on my chest. Nipples hard and sensitive, she moans and sucks my thumb harder with each graze, pinch, and full-on squeeze of her breasts.

When I twist her nipple between my thumb and fingers, her head falls back on a guttural groan that has my cock throbbing and dislodges my thumb from her mouth. Slowly, I trail my wet thumb down her neck, between her breasts, along her abdomen, stopping a moment to appreciate the dance of her muscles below her skin as she grinds her hips, rubbing her perfect cunt along my cock. The sight of me wet from her arousal has me shaking with the need to pin her to the bed, filling her balls-deep, and pounding into her as she screams my name.

Fuck. I pinch her nipples and squeeze her breasts instead, as my wet thumb meets her center, slipping through her folds to find that tight bundle of nerves.

"Oh, fu…" she gasps as she trembles, her nails biting into my chest, her mouth falling open, her face raised to the ceiling as she writhes on me, taking, taking, taking what she needs.

"Take it, Wildflower." My voice is so raw, I hardly recognize it as I'm lost to the sight of her riding me without actually *riding* me.

I imagine my need to sink inside her is as strong as her need to be filled. Her body is crying for it in every thrust of her hips, beggingly tight nipples, and needful grasps of her hands. She aches for it, driving herself forward, over and over, trying, trying, trying to be filled, stuffed full of my cock.

Not yet.

I wouldn't stop this train for the world, watching her take her pleasure in my touch, on my body, my heart right here with hers, pounding, pounding, pounding, bleeding and beating for her—only for her.

"Reid," she whines, gripping the wrist of my hand teasing her breasts. Braced, she combats whatever it is inside women that makes it hard for them to come but so blazingly spectacular when they do. "Ohmygod."

She arches.

The world stills.

My breath catches.

Her knees tremble at my sides.

Slowly, slowly, slowly I follow the goosebumps that trail along her skin. Her shoulders cave as a small whimper crosses her lips, and complete ecstasy writes the contours of her face.

"Reid." It's barely a whisper as she fights for air and her orgasm surges, surges, surges.

"So fucking beautiful," I grouse, fighting the need to move, to consume her, to take my own pleasure that will in no way match the total body release she experiences.

A woman's orgasm may be hard-earned, but the payoff is spectacular. No wonder so many people make sex tapes, if only to capture this moment of complete and all-consuming rapture.

She'd hate it.

I'd relish it and probably never stop jerking off to it.

But why jerk off to a 2D image when I have this amazing woman in real life?

"Ohmyholy—" She falls forward, breathing into my neck. "That... Reid... I have no words."

Her breath tickles, making me chuckle, making me groan as I run my hands up and down her spine, hitting that spot low on her back that makes her arch and press her hips into me. I grip her ass, my fingers exploring, slipping inside her, whispering, "Need you," against her shoulder.

Her returning moan is all the encouragement I need to roll us, her laxed body opening for me, allowing me to settle between her legs, prodding, grinding until her eyes open, her hand splaying along my cheek. "Take what you need."

Face to face, mouth to mouth, I surge home, stilling a moment to relish the way her body takes me, consumes me, wraps around me like a cocoon.

Heated and tranquil.

Strong and enticing.

Supple and ravenous.

I etch this moment into my brain, better than any photograph or video. This is the meaning of life. Not sex, but this overwhelming connection of want and need, this binding of souls and heart. My life for hers. Hers for mine.

We are one.

One.

One.

I found my other half in a flower shop. Her wavy brown hair, soulful green eyes, and her nervous stammer drew me in like a succubus. I was lost to her the moment our eyes met.

No, not lost. I was found.

"Reid," she pleads, her glorious lips sliding against mine.

I start to move, swallowing her gasps, sucking her tongue and nearly dying in the wet heat of her mouth and pussy as she takes me in to her body, loving on me like only she can.

I've nearly lost her three times now: two fires and the stupidity of secrets and fear.

No more holding back. I'm all in.

"I got you, Flower." I always have. I always will.

I'll love on my Wildflower for millennia to come, taking each day as a blessing and a gift, knowing she's right there beside me, loving me right back.

Don't forget to get Reid and Daisy's BONUS
SCENES by subscribing to my Newsletter!
https://dl.bookfunnel.com/98qjnc6pgy

ACKNOWLEDGMENTS

Thank you to all the first responders who put their lives on the line every day for people they don't even know. You are truly the bravest, the best of all of us. Thanks to you and your families who support and love you.

To my sweet family who supports me endlessly. Thank you a million times over.

Thank you to my DIVAs. Your support and love of my books and writing journey mean more than you can ever know.

To all my author friends and the book community at large, thank you for your kinship, support, and camaraderie.

Thank you to my editors, Tamara and Krista, and my PA, Ashley, for making me look like I know what I'm doing.

And last, but definitely not least, to my steady readers, I thank you for buying my books, reading my stories, and coming back for more. It still amazes me I get to do this for a living, and you are the reason why. I am blessed because of you.

Don't stop. Keep reading! And don't forget to leave a review.

Blessings, Dana

ABOUT THE AUTHOR

D.M. Davis is a Contemporary and New Adult Romance Author.

She is a Texas native, wife, and mother. Her background is Project Management, technical writing, and application development. D.M. has been a lifelong reader and wrote poetry in her early life, but has found her true passion in writing about love and the intricate relationships between men and women.

She writes of broken hearts and second chances, of dreamers looking for more than they have and daring to reach for it.

D.M. believes it is never too late to make a change in your own life, to become the person you always wanted to be, but were afraid you were not worth the effort.

You are worth it. Take a chance on you. You never know what's possible if you don't try. Believe in yourself as you believe in others, and see what life has to offer.

Please visit her website, https://dmckdavis.com, for more details, and keep in touch by signing up for her newsletter, and joining her on Facebook, Instagram, Twitter, and Tiktok.

ADDITIONAL BOOKS BY
D.M. DAVIS

UNTIL YOU SERIES
Book 1—Until You Set Me Free
Book 2—Until You Are Mine
Book 3—Until You Say I Do
Book 3.5—Until You eBook Boxset
Book 4—Until You Believe
Book 5—Until You Forgive
Book 6—Until You Save Me

FINDING GRACE SERIES
Book 1—The Road to Redemption

BLACK OPS MMA SERIES
Book 1—No Mercy
Book 2—Rowdy
Book 3—Captain
Book 4—Cowboy
Book 5—Mustang

STALK ME

Visit www.dmckdavis.com for more details about my books.

Keep in touch by signing up for my Newsletter.
Connect on social media: Reader's Group, Facebook,
Instagram, Twitter, TikTok
Follow me: Book Bub, Goodreads